A Bed Of Blood

Copyright ©June 2, 2013
by Tammy Dunning
ISBN-0992006929

Special Thanks

Without the help from my mother, this book wouldn't be nearly as good as it is. She is wonderful in so many ways. I am blessed to have had her bring me into this world to play the role of her daughter. She is my dear friend and confidant, not just my mom.

CHAPTER 1

The dawn peeks through the tiny breach in the drapes of my once-dark bedroom. My face pushes flat onto my sweat-dried sheets. My body aches when I move. I blink several times trying to shake the dizziness that lingers from the medication I took last night to try and kill off yet another of my brain-crushing migraines.

Painfully, I roll to my side so that I can swing my legs off the bed and onto the floor. I slowly sit up, rubbing my sweaty face, trying to unwrap the wayward strands of my hair that have woven themselves through my eyelashes and into my dry mouth.

At least the pain in my head has eased enough so that I'm not seeing lightning bolts across my eyes. I pull myself to my feet, wobbling only slightly due to my stiff muscles. I take a deep breath in, hoping it will disperse the tiny flickering stars in my eyes. My blood pressure must be low again.

My pajamas are clinging to my body as I walk. Mom must have closed my bedroom door last night because I always leave it open. Sometimes she can't sleep so she cleans or bakes in the middle of the night. Maybe she was preparing dough and didn't want the loud hum of the mixer to disturb me. She knew I had another migraine.

My bare feet slap the hardwood floor with every step as I make my way down the hall to the bathroom. The toilet seat it up. Odd. Mom must have been cleaning it and forgot to put it down. After I pee and flush, I spin the hot water tap, holding my hands under the gushing water, patiently waiting for the heat.

The mirror reflects my tired face with purple circles hanging below my blue, blood-shot eyes. Even my lips look swollen, for some reason. I gather my long black hair into a ponytail then wash my face and brush my teeth. Although the once greasy skin is now clean, I still look like I was run over by a bus.

The floor creaks under my feet as I make my way to the kitchen. The sunlight, shining brightly through the huge picture windows, is almost blinding. My eyes are still sensitive to the brightness of the early dawn. Each step I take down the long winding staircase seems to introduce me to a different sore muscle. My body aches so.

I fill the kettle, set it on the stove and turn on the gas. After a slight "woosh", flames flicker beneath the black pot. I seek out my huge travel mug from the cupboard then toss in a peppermint teabag. Since I spill quite often and don't want to wear hot tea on my lap, as I have on many occasions, I like to use a cup with a lid just to be safe. Even though I gulp down a big glass of orange juice, I'm still parched. Perhaps the tea will help with that.

Cup of tea in hand, I stroll over to the sliding glass doors and pull them open. It's not locked. Mom must have forgotten to lock it when she let Jack outside for his last pee of the night before she took him to bed with her.

Jack is a brown and white border collie. He's not my favorite animal in the world. He's my mom's dog, not mine and he insists on reminding me of that frequently by not listening to any commands that I give him. He's stubborn with me but nice as pie to mom and just about everyone else. He doesn't like men however. I think he does things just to irritate me. I wonder if dogs actually have that kind of mental capacity.

It's just mom and I that live here in this quaint house in the middle of nowhere, close to Herridge Lake in Temagami, Ontario. We moved here after my dad was sent to prison and my mom's first book started to sell like hot-cakes. She decided that we had enough money to disappear and start over. So this is where we came.

Where is Jack? He's usually standing at the door, glaring at me, or so I think. I turn and sip my tea while I make my way to mom's room in search of that damn dog. Maybe he didn't hear me fussing about. I really don't care if he goes outside or not but since mom sleeps late, he usually gets up with me. He pees then climbs back into bed with my mom until she gets up.

Her door is closed. That's unusual. She never closes her door unless she's changing. I knock quietly while I listen for any noise. I hear no response. She must still be sleeping. Gently and as quietly as I can, I turn the handle and push the door open. This is the exact moment when my world implodes.

She is on the bed, not moving. The floor has a shiny dark red all over it. Jack lifts his head from where he lies quietly next to mom. He looks so sad. Why? My brain can't figure out what's wrong here. It's like I'm frozen but my eyes can move, seeing the horror that lies out in front of me. I must be having a nightmare, this can't be real!

Mom lies unmoving, eyes vacant, hair disheveled. Her nightgown is torn, lying in shreds across her belly. Her breasts and her most private area are exposed. Her skin is blotched with the same matter that has soaked into the rug, the bed, spattered on the ceiling and saturated Jack's fur. He stares at me, not moving.

Finally my body moves. How long have I been standing in the doorway? I slip with each step as I slowly make my way through the ooze heading for my mother. Maybe she's all right. My body again freezes as I've reach the bed and look down at my mother.

I've discovered the source of the red. My mother lies on a bed of blood. Blood that once pumped through her veins. This is not a dream at all, this is really happening. I reach out and touch her face, but instantly pull back. Her face is so cold. I rub my hand on my pajama pants but the chill doesn't rub off. My eyes travel down her body, seeing the holes and gashes in her once perfectly pale, intact skin.

My tea cup crashes to the floor, popping the lid off and spilling hot peppermint liquid into a pool of blood. Instantly, tears fill my eyes, erupting down my cheeks, landing on my mother's dead hand. She's missing her baby finger. It's just gone. Where is it? Panic fills my body, my brain, my soul. Every nerve in my being is on fire.

Immediately I start searching for her finger; why I don't know. Perhaps if I find it and put it back on, she'll be okay. My thinking isn't reasonable. I climb onto the bed and seach around my mother's body for her missing digit. When my eyes reach her neck, I see the most horrible thing that anyone should ever have to witness. Her throat is cut so deep, that she's almost decapitated.

Suddenly my brain starts to work again, coming to the realization that even if I find her finger and try to re-attach it, I can't wake her up. My mother is dead. Someone murdered her!

I grab Jack firmly by the fur even though he disagrees and I run from the room, slipping in the crimson goo with each step. I fall face down, dropping Jack who runs from the room, leaving bloody paw prints on the hardwood floor. A foul scent of iron invades my nostrils. I crawl to the hallway, shedding tears.

A wail blasts from my chest, escaping my body. Again and again the sound of painful screams, filled with the terror that now overtakes me, rip through the house. My throat aches but I still can't stop. I pull myself to my feet and stagger to the living room, forcing myself to walk toward the phone. It seems to take a lifetime to reach that link to the outside world.

I pick up the handheld phone and punch in 911. The 9 and the 1 are now hidden behind the blood from my fingerprints.

A female voice speaks. "911 do you need police, fire or ambulance?" Silence on the line.

Confusion fills my mind. Who do I need here? I can't seem to decide. Trying to speak loudly but only managing a whisper, I say, "Everyone. I need everyone."

"Ma'am, can you tell me your name please?" The female voice sounds slightly abrupt.

"My name? I'm Katie Mason. I need help." I manage to remember my name. I think I'm on autopilot; it's the only way I can deal with this right now. I feel numb.

"Katie, how old are you?" The voice asks.

"I'm eighteen." I respond.

"Katie, my name is April. Can you tell me what the situation is?"

How do I explain what I saw when I'm not fully sure myself? "My mom is... dead, I think. No, she's dead. She's really cold. Her neck is cut really badly and there's so much blood. Please send someone quickly. I don't know what to do. What do I do?"

Panic courses through my veins but I can't react. I stand fixed in position, blood clinging to my clothes, dripping from my elbows, onto my feet. Jack is hiding behind the sofa in the corner. I think he's whimpering but I can't be sure of anything right now. I couldn't care less about that stupid mutt. Where the hell was he when someone was hurting my mother? He's a dog... it's his job to protect her. Isn't it? I hate him!

"Did you say that your mother is dead?" The operator's voice wakes me from my thoughts.

"Is someone coming?" I plead.

"The police and an ambulance are on their way. You just stay on the phone with me." April's voice is calm and assertive. I think she's the only thing keeping me from completely falling apart. "Can you tell me anything else about your situation?"

"I have blood on my pajamas." I say without really thinking.

"That's all right, you can change later." She pauses momentarily then says, "Can you make your way outside to wait for the police?"

"Okay." Without a second thought, I press the 'Off' button on the phone and place it back in its cradle. I turn and head for the front door. Outside, I stand in the sun, blood-soaked clothing, staring blankly down the long driveway as I wait for help to arrive. It's taking so long. The pain in my head is beginning to hammer at my brain again.

I close the door behind me so that Jack doesn't follow me outside, not that I would care if he ran away but he's covered in blood. I don't know why that matters. I take a few steps down the stairs then turn and look back toward the door. Bloody footprints in the exact size and shape of my feet remain painted on the stairs. They seem foreign. When I follow them with my eyes, I notice that the prints lead to me. My feet are red, red with my mother's blood. Those prints are mine.

The sun is warm on my head but the air is cold. I tilt my face upward just slightly, feeling the heat on my face. Sirens sound off in the distance. I turn my gaze down the hill toward the long road to our house. Red flashing lights sit atop a speeding SUV police vehicle followed closely by an ambulance. All those lights flashing and sirens wailing make my brain want to explode. I'm having sensory overload.

I can't catch my breath. Tiny white lights flicker like stars. The vehicles vanish. Dark takes over before I feel my body fall into the dirt below me. I am asleep, I think.

CHAPTER 2

From what seems like a hundred miles away, Jack is barking incessantly. My eyelids snap open angrily to figure out why. I see only blurs. Blinking several times doesn't seem to clear the picture. Strangely enough, I can see the bright red of my eyelids with each blink. I think I'm dreaming.

I'm in my bedroom. The posters on my wall and the white painted dresser give it away. I hear muffled voices off in the distance that sound angry. What are they arguing about? The words aren't making any sense. My eyes close but I don't leave my dream.

I hear boots in the hallway as they try unsuccessfully to be quiet. I fight to open my eyes but they just won't. Perhaps even in my dream I am medicated. I must be on my migraine medication. I hate this feeling of no self-control. My nose twitches and stings from the smell of iron in my nostrils.

A soft voice stirs me from my dream. I am quickly yanked from the bizarre fog of my thoughts, awakened to a dark-haired man in his mid twenties leaning over me.

At first I'm terrified and confused: where am I? My first thought is who the hell is this strange man and why is he in my bedroom looking at me, touching me? I fight to sit up, to get away.

"Easy! Take it easy! You're all right. You passed out. Do you remember anything?" The man smiles at me and puts his hands up in a surrendering way.

With wide eyes, desperate to understand what's happening to me, I try to speak but can't. Icy cold air is blasting at my nose and lips through a mask that is strapped to my face. In a failed attempt to take it off, I realize that I'm belted down and can't free my arms. By the swaying movements, I can tell that I'm in a vehicle of some sort.

In an effort to respond to him, I try to shake my head 'no', even though I'm pretty sure I remember how I got here but my head won't move. It is cradled in some type of restraint, holding it firmly in place. I can't help but think that all of this is so completely unnecessary.

"That's okay, don't worry about it. You're in an ambulance. I'm Steve and I'm doing what I can to help you out. Up there in the driver's seat chauffeuring us this morning is my partner. You can call him Jeremy." A sad attempt at a smile creeps up on his face.

From somewhere else in the vehicle, I hear another voice. This one is much deeper and louder than Steve's. "Yeah but name is actually Leo."

Steve's eyes laugh. I want to but I can't. Memories of this morning begin to rip through my thoughts again. I begin to cry. I silently scream because I'm too exhausted and haven't the energy required to wail. They just melt back into my body, burning my core.

Pretending not to notice, Steve checks the machines that are attached to me by cords as they make soft blipping noises and the occasional beep.

The drive seems to take forever though it can't be more than twenty minutes. Time is swallowed up when my mind shows me memories of my mom from as far back as I can remember. I see her smile when she was young. So many visions of her face flow through my thoughts, with every expression from elation to defeat and devastation.

The last time I saw her, she was sipping a glass of pink wine in front of the fire, stretched out in her recliner in her favorite old nightgown, reading the final draft of the book she had just written. My migraine was so bad that I didn't sit down to talk to her before I hurried off to bed. I was in a rush when I got off work so I could get home and take a pill for my head. I just wanted to go to sleep. I regret that I didn't take the time to treasure her. If I'd only known...

When we arrive at the hospital, everyone is fussing about me, undoing cords and tubes then plugging them in to bigger machines that make louder blipping noises. My heart starts to pound and my body begins to shake. I think I'm having a panic attack. Sweat beads cover my forehead.

Anger erupts from deep inside me and I yell, "Please, stop." Nobody acknowledges that I've even spoken. Yelling as loud as I can, I scream, "Stop! Let go of me! I'm fine. I just passed out. I'm not hurt. Now let me out of these restraints, please!"

Everyone in the room halts and looks at me. The silence is broken only by a gentle female voice. "All right. If you tell us something is hurting you, we can go from there but I need you to stop yelling and calm down or I'll have to sedate you."

As easily and smoothly as I can manage, I say, "Fine. I had a migraine last night. I passed out, that's all. Sometimes when my head hurts, I get dizzy and black out. It's no big deal. Now I'm begging you, will you let me out? I have to go see my mom."

The doctor orders the nurses to remove my restraints. They immediately follow her orders. Relief. As soon as my arms are free, I start pulling at the oxygen mask, attempting to remove it.

A nurse with long blonde hair grabs my wrist. "No honey, you have to leave that on, okay? It will help get more oxygen to your brain which will ease that migraine. Leave it on, all right?"

I nod my head but roll my eyes. I hate the way my face feels so cold with this stupid thing on. At least I can move now. That same nurse raises the upper part of my bed to a sitting position. Somehow she notices my quick smile of gratitude from underneath the mask and returns the gesture before quietly leaving the room.

The doctor puts down the chart on the small table beside my bed before pulling out a tiny, very bright flashlight and beaming it into my eyes, one at a time. I despise that, especially when I have a migraine because my eyes become sensitive to bright lights. It feels like the light is echoing through my brain, burning it from the inside out.

"Light sensitivity? Do you get migraines often?" When I nod, she writes something on the chart. "Have you ever had a shot of Demerol to ease the pain?"

"Yeah. About a year ago when I had a really bad one and it lasted for a few days. My mom brought me in here. My mom..."

Emptiness fills my chest and heavy tears once again flow from my eyes as a soft pitiful sigh escapes my throat.

The doctor, now looking at me, asks, "Did it help you?" When I look at her with confusion, she adds, "The Demerol. Did it help you?"

Still blinking trying to dissipate the white spots in my eyes from the damn light, I say, "It did but they put something in it so I wouldn't vomit. Sometimes I get sensitive to some medication and throw up."

"That's quite common to feel nauseated with medication." The doctor says to me before firing off a request to the nurse with the red hair who has been putting blankets on my legs and fussing with the machines. She hurries out of the room to fill the order.

The doctor takes my hand in hers and looks at me very seriously but also with pity. "The police are going to want your clothing for evidence. Would you like to change now or after they come and take your statement. They are waiting down the hall to speak with you."

I close my eyes only to picture my mother lying in a pool of blood, staring at the ceiling with those dead eyes. I pop mine open to try and erase the image. "I'll change now. They can have them. I want to get out of these clothes. Besides, I won't want to undress after you give me the shot."

"All right, we'll get you a gown to put on." She pats my hand with her free one. "Is there anything else I can do for you?"

Yeah, put me in a time machine so I can go back a day and save my mother's life. I shake my head. She frees my hand and pats my shoulder before strolling from the room. The nurse with the blonde hair comes back in with a small jug and a paper cup filled with ice chips. She sets them down on the nightstand before opening a cupboard, pulling out two gowns.

"Here you go, Sweetheart. Put one on with the opening at the back then put the second one on like a housecoat. Here is a bag that you can put your clothes in." She places everything down on my bed, looks at me and asks, "Do you need any help changing?"

I shake my head, "Thank you."

She leaves the room, closing the door behind her. I start with my t-shirt, so I can wrap up in the gowns before removing my pajama bottoms. I wonder for a moment if I should fold them before placing them in the paper bag. The dried patches of blood stiffen the material. I stuff them in the bag then set it down at the end of the bed before curling up under the covers.

My head pounds so hard that my muscles are starting to tense and release with each throbbing pulse in my brain. This is how I get the sore, achy body. I focus on my breathing; slow, concentrated breaths. There's a tap at the door then it opens slowly. The red haired nurse peeks in, and, realizing that I'm dressed, pushes it open.

She smiles at me easily before asking me to lift my gown so she can inject the Demerol. I hate this part, it burns slightly, never mind the hurt from the needle jamming into my rump muscle.

The doctor enters the room with a kit in her hand. She says, "The sheriff would like me to examine you for any evidence that might help solve this case. Will you allow me to process you for any possible DNA that may have been transferred onto you when you entered your mother's room?"

"How would I have DNA on me that will solve this case? Wait, do they think that I killed my mother?"

"I don't know all the particulars of this investigation. It's procedure, that's all." She steps closer to me and takes my hand. "It won't take very long."

"I'm probably going to fall sleep from the medication so I can't see why not." I pull my hand back then sit up. "Go ahead, do what you have to."

"Do I have your permission to examine you for evidence of sexual assault? From what you've told us, you were heavily medicated last night and may not be aware that you were violated." She looks at me quizzically.

"Nobody touched me. I would have known." I say quietly.

"It is possible." She says as she puts her hand on my arm to comfort me.

"I don't think so. I'm a virgin. I'm pretty sure I would hurt if someone... did that to me. And I don't, so I think I'm okay.

I don't want anyone to check that, please." I state.

She smiles at me and pats my arm. "You most likely would be sore. I'll let the detective know that you are refusing the rape kit."

My thoughts are starting to feel fluffy. Peacefulness washes over me and slowly the pain in my head becomes a distant one. Relief.

Photos are taken along with scrapings from under my fingernails and swabs from different parts of my body. I don't ask questions; I don't really care right now. She could do just about anything to me at this very moment and I wouldn't argue. The effects from the Demerol make me feel warm and fuzzy, happy and relaxed. Now I know why she asked permission before the medication kicked in. Otherwise I would have consented to anything.

After the evidence is collected, I close my eyes as I curl up with the blankets over my head, oxygen mask still blasting icy air onto my face. It's actually a welcome feeling now. I drift off to sleep.

CHAPTER 3

Mom stands in the kitchen drying her hands on the dishtowel before hanging it back on the stove handle. She smiles at me then in slow-motion, walks toward her bedroom. She turns around to look at me just as she opens her bedroom door. She pauses for a moment as the door gently swings open, with a soft creak.

"Katie, it's all up to you now. You're stronger than you think you are. Always remember that I love you." Mom turns to enter her bedroom.

"Mom, wait!" Panic consumes me and I run as fast as I can but it's just not fast enough. My feet feel like they're being sucked into mud. I fight and scream at her to not go in there. "Please, Mom, stop!"

The door closes behind her. The force pulling down on me feet lets me go and I run to her door. I fling the door open. I burst into the room. I'm too late, she's dead.

Her blood has drained from her wounds and saturated the sheets. My feet are now covered in blood. It rises up my legs as if I'm sinking in the viscous redness.

The stench of iron rankles my nose as I breathe. I try to get to my mom but I'm sinking deeper and deeper. Her blood is up at my throat and still rising. I scream for help but there is no one to pull me from my bloody grave. It consumes me. I swim as hard as I can but to no avail. I scream out my one last breath, knowing it's over.

I wake gasping for air. My hands grip the sheets as I lie there shaking, tears running down my cheeks. It was just a dream... just a horrible, frightening nightmare.

Several people are talking, their voices muffled. I think they're talking about me because I'm fairly sure that I hear someone say my name. Why are there people in my bedroom when I'm asleep? My eyes slowly open and with a slight fog still lingering from the medication, I try to figure out where I am exactly.

The room is white with an ugly striped curtain wrapped in a semi-circle around my bed. The voices I hear are coming from behind it. Two men and one woman. I've never felt more alone than I do right now. I want my mom. Sorrow overwhelms me. I realize that never again will I see her gentle face smiling at me. Never again will she hold me when I cry. Never again will we chat for hours on the sofa in front of the fireplace. Never again. Never again.

A face peeking around the curtain startles me from my thoughts. The face disappears, then one by one, the three people come out from behind the drape. The first person is the sheriff, the second is a woman that I don't recognize and the third is our towns deputy. They each have a notebook and pen in hand and sober looks on their faces. For a moment, I wonder if they've ever smiled. I would not want their jobs; too much misery.

The sheriff is a tall man and familiar to me. He steps forward and puts his right hand out for me to shake. I return the gesture. The other two just nod at me and I nod back, barely moving my head.

"Katie Mason, is that your full name?" The sheriff asks abruptly breaking the silence in the room. I tilt my head in confusion because he knows me fairly well.

"Yeah. It's actually Katie Anne Mason." I answer with a nod.

"Hi Katie, how are you feeling?" Sheriff Percy Johnson's voice is so deep that he sounds like Barry White. I know him from serving him at Foster's Cafe where I work. "I'm very sorry about what has happened to you this morning. We have been waiting for you to wake up. You were asleep for a few hours. We do have some questions for you. Are you up to it?"

"It didn't happen to me; it happened to my mother. Someone killed her but I think you already know that." What I say comes out sounding rather harsh. That was not my intent.

The sheriff clears his throat before he speaks again. "Well, yes, I am very sorry about everything that's taken place. I'm also concerned about you. Did anything happen to you?"

I shake my head. "Nobody touched me, if that's what you mean. I'm fine."

"Thank you for allowing us to take DNA evidence from your body along with photos. We were informed that you don't believe you were sexually assaulted and therefore had refused a rape kit." He clears his throat again. "Can you describe the events that took place, starting last night?

Be as detailed as you can, please." Sheriff Johnson asks while the other two prepare their paper and pens to take notes.

"I was at work at the Foster's Cafe until 10:30 last night." I close my eyes and I slowly exhale before I continue. "We close at 10:00 but we take a half hour to clean up afterward. We prepare the tables and stuff so the morning shift doesn't have to do anything but preheat the grill when they get there."

The female detective steps forward. "Katie, my name is Detective Louise Fillborn. I'm from Sudbury and was asked here to assist in this investigation because of my extensive training and knowledge in cases such as this one. I'm very sorry that you are going through this. Rest assured that we are going to work very hard to find the person or persons responsible for this crime. I need to ask you some questions. Did anything unusual occur while you were at work? Did something or someone seem out of character? Anything out of the ordinary?"

Louise is not an extraordinarily pretty woman, by any means. She has light brown hair and green eyes. By standing next to the towering six foot five Sheriff Johnson, she is dwarfed - a mere five foot four inches tall. Her clothes hang from her tiny, malnourished looking frame. Just by looking at her, it's obvious that she spends too much of her energy working and not nearly enough time on a healthy life style.

I search my memory for anything that may have seemed out of the ordinary at the cafe but come up blank. "No, nothing that didn't seem normal. We had the regulars for the dinner rush and after that just the odd truck driver here and there. It was just like any other night."

"When it was time to close the cafe, were there any people still hanging around that you had to ask to leave?" She asks me.

"Just a few people, truck drivers mostly. It's not unusual. After being alone on the road for so long, they get talking to one another and don't want to leave. None of them has ever given us any trouble." I tell her. "And before you ask, I didn't recognize any of them."

Fillborn nods her head and looks down at her paper to write something. The Sheriff nods, urging me to continue explaining what led up to me finding my mom so viciously murdered.

"I had a migraine so I couldn't wait to get home and go to bed. We cleaned up as fast as we could so we'd be able to leave sooner. I think we left just before 10:30. I drove home, parked, came in the house, got a glass of water, took my pills for the head, said 'Hi' to my mom, went pee, changed my clothes then fell asleep. It's pretty much my routine on a headache night." I remember how I didn't sit down with mom. I should have.

Sheriff Johnson asks, "When you got home and parked the car, was there anything unusual that you may have seen or heard?"

I shake my head.

The female detective asks, "Was the door locked when you came home? Like, did you have to use your key or did your mom let you in"

"I just walked in. Mom doesn't lock it when I'm expected home. There's not much reason to secure the doors around here. We usually lock up when we go to bed at night but rarely during the day. There are no houses for half a mile one way and the highway is about half a mile the other way, so there really isn't much need to. We're pretty safe where we live... Or at least, we thought we were." A cold shiver runs through me and if I wasn't still numb from the shot of Demerol that I got earlier, I'd probably burst into a puddle of tears.

Johnson asks, "Nothing unusual... Okay so, when you came in the house, what happened then?"

"Mom was sitting in her recliner in front of the fire. She asked me if I could sit for a little while. She said she wanted to talk to me about something. We talk a lot, so it's not unusual. She probably wanted to talk about how messy my room has been lately." I wish I could still hear her nag me about cleaning it. Just once more. "Look, nothing happened any different than any other night. Everything was normal, like every other day." A thought passes through my mind and my face must show something that interests the sheriff. He looks like he's trying to read my mind.

"What are you thinking, Katie?" He asks.

"My dreams from last night, they weren't like normal dreams." I take a moment to recall the details. "I heard clunky footsteps, like heavy work boots on the hardwood floor. Someone closed my door. Mom rarely does and if so she opens it before she goes to bed. But it was shut when I woke up this morning. I remember dreaming of voices; yelling or speaking loudly, I can't be sure. Everything is so foggy from my medication. It makes it really difficult to focus and be clear. Dreams seem real sometimes. Kind of like right now. It doesn't feel like I'm awake. I just want to sleep."

After writing something on his pad and taking a few steps toward the window, peeking through the blinds, he says, "Perhaps we should let you rest and pick it up when you're feeling better."

Detective Fillborn asks, "I have just one more question, if you don't mind. When you woke up this morning, was there anything else that struck you as odd, like a door being left unlocked, a window open, or something moved, missing...?"

I think back through the fog of this morning's memories. "Yeah, the toilet seat was up and the back door was unlocked. My mom's door was closed too. I thought she was sleeping so I opened it to get Jack so he could go outside to pee."

She asks, "Does your mom usually close her door at night?"

"No, never. She leaves it open so Jack can drink through the night. That's what she always does... did." My insides twist and ache for my mother.

"Okay, that's all for now. You need to rest." The Sheriff nods his head as he tries to usher his detectives out of the room. "We'll speak again soon. You just worry about getting yourself better. Let us work on the rest." He pats my leg as he leaves the room ahead of his colleagues.

Deputy River Walters is the third person in the room. He comes into the diner quite a bit. Being twenty-three and single, he doesn't spend a lot of time at home cooking for himself. He's a good looking guy: 6'2" tall, blonde hair, eyes jade, built strong, lean and athletic. The brightness of his smile could light up the darkest night.

A lot of the girls in town are crazy about him but he doesn't date. He just says that he enjoys being single. We all thought that maybe he was gay until we saw him mesmerized over a *Sports Illustrated* Swimsuit Edition about a year ago.

He's been very quiet up until now which isn't unusual for him. He doesn't have too much to say most of the time. He's what my mom calls 'a deep thinker'. Nobody really knows all that much about him. He just moved to town one day and the next thing I knew, he was the Deputy Sheriff. He doesn't talk much, only when he has something important to say.

"Katie, I'm truly sorry about all this. I really am. If there's anything I can do, don't hesitate to call." He smiles shyly before quickly leaving the room.

I close my eyes and try to drift back to sleep so I can leave all of this terror behind me, even if only for a little while. I let the fog of the Demerol take over me. Sleep comes quickly.

CHAPTER 4

I hear my mother's voice, talking loudly from downstairs. I wonder who she's talking to. I can't make out the mumbling voice that seems to follow hers as she walks through the house. There is a man with her. His voice is muffled through the floorboards.

It's late at night, or very early in the morning, I can't tell. The sun isn't peeking through my blinds. My vision isn't clear so the numbers on my clock are blurry. The people sound like they're talking from inside a bubble. I hear my mother shriek.

I awake with a gasp. I turn to see Mrs. Foster, standing with her back to me, staring out the window. It's nearly dark outside. I must have slept all day. It doesn't seem as though it were just this morning that I found my mother murdered in her bed, it feels like it's been days.

"Mrs. Foster?" I call out to her, letting her know that I'm awake. My throat is so dry that a whisper is all I can manage.

She starts, spinning around quickly to look at me, her eyes sad. She wipes her face with a tissue to remove the trails of tears that streak her face, then gently blows her nose. She stands in a very proper manner with her chin held high as she straightens her clothing before slowly walking to my bedside.

I can tell she's trying to gather her thoughts on what she's going to say to me simply by how stiffly she moves. I've never seen her so emotional. I truly didn't think she cared very much about me and she hardly knew my mother.

Mrs. Foster has never been a very motherly type of person to me. She has always kept me at arm's length. She is my boss. When she takes my hand in hers, I am reminded that something is horribly wrong.

"Katie, I'm very sorry for what has happened." I can see her searching for her next words. "I'm not sure what to say. Mr. Foster and I are here for you if you need us... for anything. I know that I don't show it but I've come to care a great deal for you. It pains me that you are going through this. Can I get you anything?"

She's never been at a loss for words around me. It's unnerving. "Water?" I manage to ask.

She pours a cup of water for me from the blue jug on my bedside table. It's not very cold but I'm thankful just the same. I hand it to her empty and she refills it quickly before returning it to me.

This time I don't drink it right away. "Why are you here?" I ask but realize immediately that I've insulted her. "I'm sorry. What I meant to say was thank you for coming but how did you find out I was here?"

"Like every morning, the sheriff was having his breakfast in the cafe with his deputy when the call came out over his radio. I was refilling his coffee cup at the time and overheard. The voice was telling him to go to the Mason home because someone's carrying on about a murder."

"So did everyone hear the call go out?" I ask.

"Not many people heard it but those who did began to spreading the word to those who hadn't. The exaggerated stories started very shortly afterward but I don't care much to listen in on that." She's right, she hates rumors. "I just did what I could to put it out of my mind and concentrate on the customers until I knew for sure that something drastic had indeed happened. I remember asking you before you left last night if you would come in to help with the morning rush and you said that you would be there. When you didn't show up for your morning shift at nine o'clock, that's when I knew something was definitely wrong. I called the sheriff and he told me what had happened. He suggested I come and sit with you. I didn't hesitate, of course."

"How long have you been here? What time is it?" I ask while looking around for a clock.

"It's just past seven o'clock in the evening. I've been here since about ten this morning. I didn't want to leave because I thought it would be best if you to had a familiar face to see when you woke up." She explains.

"You can turn on the lights if you'd like." I say before I gulp down the cup of water. Mrs. Foster walks over and flips up the light switch, filling the pale room with light.

"Mr. Foster and I would like to open our home to you as a place to stay until you figure out what to do next. It'll be one less thing for you to stress over in such an overwhelming time. We can provide you with everything you need until you get back on your feet." Mrs. Foster says as she nears my bedside and places her hand on mine in yet another uncomfortable motherly gesture.

"I'd rather just go home, but thank you." I say, pulling my hand from hers. I pretend that I simply need it to help myself sit up because having her touch me doesn't feel right. The situation just seems so much more real and desperate by her acts of kindness.

She slides her hand down to meet her other one and cups them together. She seems to be very uncomfortable, not quite sure what to say next. "You can't. The sheriff and the detectives are still searching it for evidence. It's a crime scene. Besides, wouldn't you be more comfortable somewhere else? I mean, after what you saw this morning, I'm sure you don't ever want to go back there."

"Why wouldn't I want to go back there? That is my home. It's where I live." I'm confused. I love my house, so did my mother. She wouldn't want me to leave because of this. She would want me to be happy and she knows that house makes me happy, or at least, it used to.

"Well, until the sheriff releases it, you'll have to stay somewhere. Do you have any relatives that we can call for you? Katie, you do realize that you'll need a place to go. Perhaps you have a girlfriend that you'd like us to call?" She asks, looking a little insulted that I'm not accepting her gracious offer.

"I'm sorry. That was mean of me. I don't want to sound ungrateful. I just want to go home. All of my clothes are there and..." My voice drifts off.

Mrs. Foster smiles and pats my shoulder, trying to comfort me. "The detective brought you some clothes to wear and a few things she thought you'd need for the next day or two. I put them on the chair over here." She sighs heavily. "Just tell me what I can do to help you through this awful time."

I shake my head. "I don't know. I'm not sure what to do. None of this seems real. It is really happening though, isn't it?" Maybe I'm hoping that she'll tell me that it's just a joke or that I'm having a nightmare but she does neither.

"Is there anyone that I can call for you?" She asks again, avoiding my question.

"Yes, can you call Billy Staple? His family knows me well and they'll take care of me tonight."

"The Staples have been sitting in the waiting room most of the day as well. You get dressed and I'll go ask the nurse to bring you the paperwork. You can sign yourself out of the hospital. I'll tell the Staple family that you'd like to see them." She hands me the bag of clothes then clears her throat. "If you change your mind at any time about accepting my offer to stay with us, please don't hesitate to call. And don't worry: I've already covered your shifts for the next week. Call me if you need more time." She pats me one more time before heading for the door.

"Wait. Where's Jack?" I ask her but she looks as me like she doesn't know who I'm talking about. "My mom's dog, Jack. Do you know where he is?"

"Oh, yes, I was told that he was sent to the town veterinarian so they could take care of him. He has a few injuries that needed surgery. He was also checked for evidence. I don't have any more details," she says before leaving the room, closing the door behind her. I don't think she likes dogs very much. I like dogs, just not Jack.

I barely have enough time to put my clothes on when Billy comes barrelling through the door, scooping me up in a big hug. His arms are wrapped around me so tightly that I can't squirm away.

"Katie, are you all right? I wanted to come and sit with you but they wouldn't let me in your room while you were sleeping." He releases me. "I tried to tell them that I'm your best friend but they didn't care. I suppose in their world boys and girls can't possibly be best friends without an agenda on the guy's part. Maybe they thought I would molest you while you were unconscious."

Mr. Staple calmly says, "It's just protocol." I'm hugged by both him and Billy's mother. "You will stay with us and I won't take no for an answer."

"Of course you're going to stay with us." Billy announces, not giving me a say.

"I'd like that. Thank you. It'll only be until they let me back in my house." I start to smile but I'm distracted.

Billy's father wraps his arms around his weeping wife while whispering something in her ear. It must have helped because she's able to gather herself, or at least pretend to be in control of her emotions for my benefit. She wipes the wetness from her cheeks and forces a smile on her face.

Billy looks at me and jokingly says, "She's a bit of a drama queen." Under normal circumstances I might laugh at that but not today. She is within her right to cry in this situation.

"Mrs. Foster said that you've all been here most of the day. You didn't have to come. I would have called. Did the sheriff ask you to come?"

Billy shakes his head. "No. I went to the cafe to see if you wanted to hang out after your shift but your car wasn't there. I thought that maybe you slept through your alarm. I tried to call your cell phone and it went to voicemail so I drove to your house.

When I saw all the cop cars and yellow tape, I knew something was really wrong. One of the cops told me what happened."

"I can't believe they would just tell you. Isn't there some rule or something?" I mutter.

"Not in a small town, I'm afraid. Nothing this noteworthy has ever happened around here before. People can't wait to spout about it." He hands me my shoes. "This place is depressing as hell. Let's get out of here."

CHAPTER 5

Naked before the full size bathroom mirror, I am shocked at the blood that has dried on my flesh. There are streaks of clean skin where someone made an attempt at washing it off. It's in my hair, matting it in knots. I see brown patches on my face, neck, arms, chest, legs and feet. I have evidence of my mother's butchery all over me. I don't really want to wash off the only thing that still links me to her because then she'll be gone, forever. But I realize that this is blood, just blood. It smells of iron, looks horrifying and makes my skin feel stiff and itchy. I cannot stay like this forever.

I watch as the hot water washes my mother's blood from my skin. It flows down me, circling the drain before disappearing, never to be seen again... much like my mother's life.

After I've dressed in my pajamas, I join Billy and his parents in the kitchen. Even though it's well past dinnertime, Mrs. Staple puts a bowl of chili, two buns and a can of pop in front of me after I sit at the dinner table. She's insisting that I eat something. Even though I haven't eaten all day, I hadn't realized that I was hungry. My stomach growls when I get a whiff of the rich and spicy chili.

Billy's father is reading a book about mental illness while his mother tidies the kitchen. Billy is finishing up some homework. Everyone is silent while I consume every bite. The house is eerily quiet. Not much is said about what happened until I've finished.

Mrs. Staple sits across from me at the table and breaks the silence. "Katie, you know that you're welcome to stay as long as you'd like. We are here for you every step of the way. You are not alone in this. If you need anything, just want to talk or simply need someone to sit beside you and not say a word... we're not going to leave you."

"Thank you, Mrs. Staple. I am grateful for everything." I say in a bare whisper.

"Do you have any family that you'd like me to call? Should we..." She swallows before finishing her sentence. "Should we contact your father?"

I shake my head. "Absolutely not! He doesn't have the right to know anything about me or my mom."

I squeeze my eyes shut, trying to shake the image of my father choking the very breath from my mother. He is a violent man. So many times, he hurt my mom. But the Staples know very little about my past.

I remember coming home from school one day when I was seven years old and walking in on my father raping my mother. He was holding her down, face first on the cold, wood floor. Her eyes were barely slits, swollen from the slaps that he gave her. He was on her, hurting her. She was fighting back the screams so as not to excite him more.

He enjoyed inflicting pain on her. He looked at me. He knew I was standing there, but he didn't stop what he was doing until he was finished. I remember the embarrassed, humiliated look on my mother's face when she realized that I was home and that I saw what he did to her. At the time I didn't understand what he was doing but I understood how badly he was hurting her. I hate that man, father or not, he's a bastard and should be dead.

"But he's your father, Katie." Mrs. Staple says.

Billy knows that I never talk about my father or what it was like to live with him. He only knows that I hate the man but not why. He says to his mom, "No Mom, just leave him out of it. He's not in her life anyway, never really was there for her. She'll be fine with us. We can be her family now."

She replies, "Yes, I know he's never been around. Of course we'll be her family... I just thought that she should have someone that's blood related." She looks to me and says, "Perhaps one day you'll let him know."

I don't understand why she believes that he has any rights to anything that involves us. I have made it clear that I hate the man. But then again, they don't know the whole truth about him. I've never told them. I've never told anybody.

My mom and I ran from him as soon as we could. He went to prison for killing a man in a bar. We were finally free from his violence. He was going away for a long time. Shortly after, my mother wrote a bestselling book series that really took off, giving us enough money to run. She said that she started writing to keep her mind off of him.

Two years ago, we closed our eyes, pointed to a place on the map and moved to it. This house was for sale and was absolutely perfect. This town seemed like a wonderful dream; quiet, easy.

My mom had enough anxiety through her life, so the gentleness of a small town was exactly what she needed. She stayed home most of the time, loving the solitude. She was truly happy here.

I say with anger, "I don't even want him to know where I am." He never hurt me but I was a child then. Things might be different now that I'm grown. He's only been in prison for six years. He has another thirteen to go. By then, he can't touch me.

Mrs. Staple nods before taking my dishes and leaving Billy and me alone. Billy is my best friend, has been for the past two years. I wasn't accepted by the other kids at the high school. I was considered an outsider because I wasn't born here.

Billy moved here six months before me. He was an outcast too. When I moved here, he took me under his wing, so to speak. We've been like two peas in a pod ever since.

"Katie, I'm really sorry. I don't know what to say. Tell me what to do and I'll do it. I just don't understand how anyone could hurt your mom. I mean, she was the sweetest, nicest person I have ever met. She was an amazing woman and she really loved you very much. I'm sorry that you're hurting so badly." He says, with a smile that doesn't reach his eyes.

"Thank you, Billy. Yeah, I don't get it. Why would anyone want to hurt my mom?" I know he doesn't have any answers for me and it's not like I expect him to give me one.

He shrugs his shoulders while reaching to take my hands in his. Instead, I lean in and bury my face in his neck and shoulder wrapping my arms around his chest. He wraps his arms around me and my emotions let loose, spilling tears onto his shirt. Wails of pain slip from my throat. It feels so good to give in to the heartache. Billy just holds me, allowing me to let it all out. He loved her too. I am safe in his arms.

We sleep together on the pull-out sofa bed in the den that Mrs. Staple made up for me. She knows that he and I aren't boyfriend and girlfriend. Letting him hold me while we sleep isn't a concern for her. We are best friends, that's all.

Through the night, Billy wakes me several times, shaking me away from my nightmares. He brushes the hair from my sweaty face and holds me tight until I fall back to sleep.

It's a long, scary night for me. I keep seeing a figure at the door of my bedroom; a man. I don't know who he is. He's just a black shadow with a light radiating from behind him, making it impossible to see his facial features.

He slowly shuts my door. That's when I scream because I know he's going to kill my mother, or already has. Is it just a bad dream or is it a memory? Is it possible that in my medication induced stupor, I actually saw my mother's killer? Before I can find out, Billy shakes me awake. I dream the same dream several times before morning finally comes to free me from the torturous night.

I wake to find Billy still holding me. "Hi, how long have you been awake?" I ask him in a raspy voice.

"Most of the night. I've been watching you sleep. You didn't sleep well so I wanted to stay awake and ward off your the bad dreams. Are you okay? Did your dreams reveal anything?" Billy asks as he releases me from his hold.

I groan as I roll onto my back and stare up at the stucco ceiling. "No, nothing new. Thank you for waking me up when I was having nightmares. I'm so glad you were here for me. I owe you one."

Billy exhales with a grunt. "Yeah, well you owe me more than one, Katie. That list is a long one. And don't think I'm not keeping track." He starts to laugh. He pulls himself out of bed while scratching his head and stretching his back. "Do you want to tell me what you were dreaming?"

I roll out of bed as I recall my nightmare. We pull the sheets off the bed and prepare to fold it back up while I describe my night terrors with as much detail as I can remember.

"I saw a man in my doorway. I don't know who he was because of the light behind him. He stood there with his arms crossed for a minute or so, just looking at me. He pulled my door shut without a sound. I don't think he knew that I saw him."

Billy stares at me, totally intrigued while he shakes the pillow out of its case before tossing it onto the sofa and the case on the pile of sheets. "Do you think it's real? I mean is it a memory from that night or do you think it's just your unconscious mind making stuff up?"

I gather the sheets in my arms and follow him to the laundry room where we drop them in a basket. "I don't know. I see the room and him in a haze just like I always see things when I'm drugged with my migraine meds. It looks the same as it would have been that night so maybe it is a memory and not just a dream. It feels so real. What do you think? Am I nuts?"

He leads the way to the kitchen where his mom is cooking breakfast and his dad is sitting at the table with his newspaper and coffee. He lowers the paper enough so he can look over it and address me.

The man tilts head down so he can look over his glasses to see me better, and says, "Good morning, Katie. Did you sleep well?"

"Good morning. Actually I didn't. I had nightmares all night. The bed was great and I'm really glad that Billy was there to wake me when I couldn't wake myself." I answer him as best I can.

I like his dad but he makes me a little nervous sometimes. Perhaps that's because I didn't have a very good male role model growing up and was not comfortable around my own father. I feel as though he's assessing me all the time. Maybe that's because he's a psychiatrist.

The phone rings, startling me and I yelp loudly enough to make everyone else jump. Billy rubs my back to ease my nerves. I smile at him, embarrassed. His mom answers the phone and after a lot of 'yeses', 'okays' and a final 'no problem, we'll bring her in after breakfast', she returns to the table and her cup of coffee.

"Katie that was Deputy Walters. He asked if we could bring you to their office because they have a few questions for you. Would that be all right?" Billy's mom asks me even though she knows that she already promised that she'd take me, so asking me is pointless.

"What about school? I have to go to school. Besides, I don't know what I can tell him that's any different than what I've already told them."I try to imagine everything going back to normal but the memories flood back with a shudder, destroying all hope.

Mrs. Staple shakes her head in protest. "No, absolutely not. You are not going to school today and neither is Billy. You two are going to spend the day together so that you can have someone you trust as your support. Anyway, I already informed the school that you both won't be attending."

We finish breakfast. I help clean up then change out of my pajamas into the jeans and sweatshirt that someone packed for me. Whoever it was forgot to grab my deodorant. Great! Maybe Billy will let me use his; it's better than nothing.

CHAPTER 6

Deputy Walters ushers me into a little room with nothing more in it than a table with four chairs around it. There is a camera up in the corner near the ceiling pointing directly at where I am to sit. Billy demands to come in with me. I hadn't thought to ask if he could come in too. After some protest, the deputy allows him in.

Deputy Walters stands in the corner beneath the camera, leaning against the wall. Louise Fillborn, the detective I met at the hospital, along with Sheriff Johnson stroll into the room, shutting the door behind them. They each take a seat, Detective Fillborn sitting closest to me.

She speaks first. "Good morning Katie. Billy, it's nice to meet you." We exchange pleasantries.

She puts a folder down in front of her and opens it up. On the inside flap of the folder is a picture of my mom and me. It must have been taken from the house because it used to sit on the mantel in a nice gold frame. Anger constricts my stomach at her nerve - taking whatever she wants! I will get that picture back.

"I have a few questions for you, if you feel up to it." She asks me as if I have a choice. I nod. "All right. You must have taken a lot of medication to have been so unconscious that you didn't hear anything. I have a hard time believing that you heard nothing. Your mother was brutally murdered, and going by the evidence, she fought her attacker with everything she had. It had to have made quite a commotion. Are you sticking to your statement that you heard nothing?"

"No, I did hear voices but they were muffled and hazy but I only remember a little bit of arguing. I tried to get up to see who was there but I couldn't do it. My drugs pretty much knock me out. Not a whole lot will wake me after I take them. My migraines can get pretty severe sometimes. Those meds are the only things that help." I answer her but do regret having taken the drugs at all that night. "If I only had of taken something else, like acetaminophen, I could have helped her."

The detective writes something on her papers then asks me, "Katie, I have to ask this question; did you murder your mother or have any knowledge of or take part in her death?"

I stare at her in disbelief. How can she ask me that question? I loved my mother with everything that I am. She was the only person in my life that truly mattered, other than Billy, of course. My blood is boiling. The rage I feel at her question is just too much and I boil over.

"What the hell are you talking about? Murder my own mother? Are you serious? How can you even think that I'd be able to do that, or want to? Oh my God! Lady, what's wrong with you?" I take a deep breath to try and calm myself. "No, I did not kill my mother and I had no part in it!"

Billy is also furious. "Do you really have to ask that? I mean, seriously. If you had seen the relationship between her and her mother, you'd never doubt for a second that Katie loved her mom deeply and could never hurt her."

"I'm sorry but it is protocol. We do need to rule you out. Most murders of this magnitude are committed by someone close to the victim. So when we investigate, we start with the closest person and work our way out from there." Fillborn, straightforward and with no emotion defends her questioning tactics.

After taking several breaths to ease my rage, I composedly say, "I just need you to know that I would never, could never, ever do anything like that to anyone, even a perfect stranger, let alone my mother. She was all I had." I blink several times in an ill-fated attempt to fight back the tears from welling up in my eyes. Slowly tears drip down my cheeks.

Sheriff Johnson reaches across the table and puts his hand over mine to console me. He's usually so business-like that he keeps his emotions at bay; strictly to the point, strong and tough. It seems weird to have him hold my hand.

"It'll be okay, Katie" Sheriff speaks as softly as his rough voice can manage. "We don't honestly believe that you had anything to do with her murder. But we did have to ask. Is there anyone that you can think of that we should investigate? Anybody at all that just didn't quite sit right with you that you think we should talk to? Did something happen recently that strikes you as odd? Did your mom mention anything or anyone?"

I think for several minutes while everyone waits quietly for my response. "Well, it's not something that's too unusual,

I mean, it happens from time to time. A trucker knocked on our door around nine o'clock one night because his truck broke down on the highway and his CB radio wasn't working. Mom let him use our phone to call someone. He left shortly after. I was at work so I didn't see him. But that was about week ago. As far as I know, he never came back."

Detective Fillborn cuts in. "Did your mom happen to say what he looked like or who he drives for? Did she give any details at all?"

"Um, no not really. She just said that he seemed like a nice guy; pleasant, polite... clean. She said he wasn't scruffy or unkempt." I say, wishing that I had asked my mom more about that stranger in the night.

"Is there anyone else?" Sheriff Johnson asks.

"I don't think so." A thought pops in my head. "She did say something to me that didn't seem like anything at the time but strikes me as odd now. It was about a month ago. She told me to be careful of people and to not assume that someone is trustworthy just because of their reputation. She made me promise not to accept rides home from work with anyone other than her. I asked her why but she just pursed her lips and made me promise. I know that she was doing a lot of research for a new book that she was working on. At the time, she was almost finished it, only a few more chapters to go. She wouldn't let me read this book as she was writing it, which is weird too. I usually read and critique her work for her as it's coming along."

Deputy Walters asks, "Did she do her research on her computer?"

"Yes, she did. She went to town a few times to look up old records from people's lives and their deaths. Like I said, I don't know what she was working on but it must have been pretty important to her. She seemed anxious, like she stumbled onto something that scared her. I wish I would have been more persistent when I asked her for more information." Regret is a horrible thing and it's starting to eat at me. "I knew something was bothering her because she'd stare off into space for long periods of time. I'd ask her what's wrong but she'd only say that it's nothing and smile at me. She seemed distracted. Maybe she was just thinking about the book she was writing."

"I will go through her computer to see what I can find out. Her history might give us an idea of what she's been working on. Even if she deleted the history, I can still track where she's been." Deputy Walters is a computer geek? Who knew?

Detective Fillborn looks at the deputy, inquiring. "Do you work with computers a lot? If you don't really know what you're doing, you could erase the history altogether and then we'll never know. I can send it off to Ottawa for the techs to go through it but it may take some time to get any information that could be useful right now, since they are usually back-logged."

"Yes ma'am. I do know about computers. I am trained in computer forensics and would not offer my services if I wasn't. This is a big investigation and I would not do anything to impede it." The deputy looks slightly irritated at her skepticism.

"All right then. You should take a look as soon as possible and let me know what you discover. Thank you, Deputy Walters. We will ship it off to the lab after you go through it. It would be quicker if we didn't have to wait for the technicians findings." She says but still looks a bit doubting of his computer skills. I do believe she will be doing a background check on him just as soon as she can.

Sheriff Johnson clears his throat then asks, "Katie is there anything else that you think might be relevant? Was there a smell that seemed out of place, like cologne?"

"No, I don't think so. All I could smell was blood; that horrible metallic odour... I could actually taste it. It was so pungent. When I close my eyes, not only can I still see her but the sting of her blood in my nose... it's so strong that I can still taste it. When will that go away?" I ask the sheriff.

"I don't know if it ever will, Katie. I still see her when I close my eyes too. I've never had to witness a murder like that before and I hope I never have to again. I am real sorry, Katie. I truly wish that this had never happened." Sheriff Johnson's expression says it all. He speaks the truth about how it's affected him. Her murder is really testing his faith in the goodness in humankind. I can see the pain in his eyes. I wonder if I appear the same way.

"So can you tell me what happened? I just need to know if she suffered horrendously. Did she feel every stab wound? I will never forget how she looked on the bed. Just tell me what happened. It can't be worse than I imagine. Please, please tell me everything." This is going to hurt. I inhale breath so I can try to prepare for what they're about to tell me.

Sheriff Johnson nods at Detective Fillborn when she looks at him questioningly. She looks down at her papers and starts sorting through them slowly. She clears her throat. "This is just our initial assessment. The victim, I'm sorry, your mother, was first struck in the face in the living room. There is evidence of blood droplets on the floor and coffee table. We believe that she was then carried to her bedroom. She was then raped, beaten and stabbed. Evidence shows that the blade penetrated twenty seven times, not consecutively. Each stab wound was spread out throughout the attack. The evidence proves that the entire act lasted for nearly two hours before she succumbed to her injuries."

Fillborn looks up from her papers to examine my reaction. I sit stone-faced, refusing to show her any emotion. If I do, I fear she will not share the rest of the information and if I'm going to help solve this thing, I need to know everything.

Meanwhile, inside of me, my inner-voice is screaming at the tops of her lungs, wailing in pain, covering her ears as she cowers in the fetal position on the floor. I swallow hard then nod my head for her to continue.

Sheriff Johnson speaks before she does, "Now Katie, that doesn't necessarily mean that she felt everything. She may have passed out. We can only hope." I think he said that to make me feel better but his eyes are too shifty for his words to be true.

She looks down at her papers once again and begins to read off evidence. "The autopsy shows that she was still alive and possibly conscious when her throat was cut. The wound was so severe that she was nearly decapitated." She takes a deep breath, letting it out slowly, shuffling in her seat as though she's uncomfortable. Her eyes lift from the paper but never reach mine. I sit perfectly still, staring at the wall in front of me. "At some point, during or after the attack, the perpetrator climbed the stairs to close your door. Going by a few blood droplets on the floor in your doorway, we believe that he stood there before closing your door. Your mother's office was ransacked. Whoever did this was looking for something that was obviously very important to him. We found her computer hidden under her mattress. Do you have any idea why she would hide it?"

I shake my head. Silence settles in the room while I sit nonreactive to the facts that she just spelled out to me. I hold my breath.

I don't think I'm feeling anything, physically or emotionally. Perhaps I'm numb again. It's probably for the better.

I finally turn my eyes toward Sheriff Johnson. "Is there anything else that you need me for today?" I come across sounding apathetic.

He looks confused, perhaps wondering why I haven't fallen apart. He stutters. "Uh, no, no not right now. You can leave if you'd like. We can find you later if we have any other questions. Will you be staying at Billy's?"

"Actually, I'd like to go home. When can I do that?" I ask, emotionless.

He looks at Detective Fillborn but she just shrugs her shoulders. "Well, ah, I suppose we'll pull out of there by later tonight but we'll need to get someone to clean it up before you'll want to go in. Aside from the obvious blood evidence, there's also black dusting powder everywhere because we were searching for fingerprints. And before you ask, we did find some but we need to run them through the Automated Fingerprint Identification System. It'll help us weed people out. When you get a chance, can you sit down and write out a list of anyone who's been to your house, inside or out, within the last few months and why they were there? That will help us out."

I stand quickly and start toward the door. "Yeah, I can do that. I'll have that for you tomorrow." Before I can reach the door, Deputy Walters already has it open for me. Billy follows closely behind.

Deputy Walters puts his hand on my shoulder as I go to pass him, then quickly removes it as if he's nervous about touching me. "If you need anything, don't hesitate to call me, all right?" He writes something on his business card and hands it to me. "My personal phone number."

"Thanks." I say as I take the card from him. "Oh wait, is there any chance that I can get my mom's day planner? All of her contacts are in there and I need to let them know what happened. Her agent doesn't even know yet."

He diverts his eyes from mine. "Yeah sure, I can look into that for you. I think we took it for evidence but I can photocopy it for you. Would that be good enough?"

"Yes, thank you. That would be great. When can I come pick that up?" I ask him.

"I'll get it to you as soon as possible. I can drop it off at the Staple residence so you don't have to go out of your way. It's not a problem." He says while still looking around the room at everything but my eyes. He's strange sometimes. He whispers quietly enough so I can hear but nobody else can. "We can arrange for you to stay at the motel here in town if you would prefer. You don't have to stay with anyone. You are eighteen so you're legally an adult."

I shake my head. "I'm good at Billy's." I nod, thanking him once more before Billy and I exit the police station. We quietly walk to his beat up old car. All I can think about is that I want to go home but first I have to go see about my mom's stupid dog, Jack.

CHAPTER 7

Billy and I enter the veterinarian's office only to be greeted by sympathetic faces. I don't much like it. We walk to the counter where a young receptionist greets us. Her name tag says 'Janet'. Looking as if she's about to cry, she forces her lips into a smile. I beg silently for her to keep the water-works at bay, at least until I'm gone.

"Jack is ready for you. I'll just have you step into this exam room. You can wait here while I get the vet and Jack for you." She leads the way to the tiny room then shuts the door behind us. She leaves through the other door that leads to the back of the building where they hold the dogs and do all their surgeries. The general public isn't supposed to be back there.

Several minutes pass before the short, chubby vet enters the room, holding Jack's chart. Even though he's in his forties, he has a cherub-like face. Judging by the laugh lines around his eyes, I can tell he's a generally happy person, but not today. "Hi Katie, we are all so very sorry to hear about your mother. How are you holding up?"

"I'm okay." I lie. Admitting that I'm feeling as though a part of me has died won't lighten the tension in this place. All that will do is bring on more tilted heads and sad faces. That won't help my struggle to hold it together and not fall to the floor in a snivelling mess.

"I'm Dr. Messley. We all feel awful about what's happened. If there's anything we can do, just let us know. We are going to absorb the cost for all the care that's needed for Jack's recovery. It's not going to cost you anything. It's the least we can do." He takes a moment before clearing his throat and getting to the matter at hand, that idiot dog. "Okay then, Jack had a few cuts and one stab wound on his right shoulder. He must have tried to stop the attacker but after he was stabbed, he wouldn't have been able to walk on that leg, let alone defend your mother. There was blood in his teeth and under his gums so it was swabbed for evidence. Now obviously we don't know if it was the attacker's blood or if it belonged to your mother or Jack himself. Let's hope that he was able to get in a good chomp in before he was incapacitated. It would be wonderful if we caught the perpetrator by the DNA evidence taken from Jack, however, the blood will most likely be your mother's. Dogs lick their young at birth so as to arouse them. This is an instinctual behavior that they transfer to humans in desperate times, in an attempt to awaken their unconscious masters."

I interrupt him because I can't stand here while I get a lecture on dog behaviour and how it might just catch the evil son-of-a-bitch that murdered my mom. He must know that I was at the murder scene, and I saw what Jack looked like that morning. "He was covered in blood when I picked him up from the bed. Is he able to walk now?"

"Oh yes, he can but he does have a limp and most likely will for the rest of his life. It won't be quite so obvious once he's healed. He's in a lot of pain right now. Part of the muscle in his shoulder was missing so we did what we could to repair it but I don't think he'll be running any marathons in the future." The vet gives a slight smile at his comedic relief, which I don't find all that funny, but I suppose nothing will seem humorous for a while. Not for me anyway.

"So he did try to help my mom?" I ask feeling guilty for thinking the worst of Jack, hating him for his cowardly behaviour in not ripping out the throat of her attacker.

"He most certainly did." He puts the chart down on the counter then heads toward the door. "How about I go get Jack for you?"

Dr. Messley barely gets the door open when Janet walks in with Jack in tow. She tries to coax him into the room. He's limping badly on his front leg. Jack looks up and notices me standing here. He stops moving and will not walk through the doorway. The vet bends down and gently picks him up with a grunt, then places him atop the examination table. Jack sits, staring at me. His eyes are sad, hopeless. I've never seen him look so vulnerable.

I don't go to him until the doctor calls me over to the table. "I need to show you his wounds so that you can look after them. You'll need to dab this cream onto the scar once a day, best time to do it is at night. He also needs to take these pills twice a day. It's an antibiotic. Here are some pills for pain as well. He can have one every eight hours if needed." The vet hands me Jack's medicine in a small plastic bag.

Dr. Messley looks at me strangely when I don't reach out to touch Jack; not to comfort him or inspect his wounds. I just stand there, hands at my sides. Jack shuffles his body so he can lean his head against me. That's when I realize it's just him and me from now on. He is no longer my mother's dog, he is mine. He needs me.

His eyes are glassy, like he's about to cry. It's almost as though an unspoken truth is shared between us; one that says our mom is dead. Tears form in my eyes to match his. I wipe them away with my sleeve before they fall hoping nobody notices. I fight the urge to look back at the dog's face to see if he is shedding tears. I will fall apart if I see him cry. I have to hold it together.

Is it possible for dogs to have emotions like we do? Can they cry like humans do? Was a silent message just relayed between us? We miss her, both of us. For the first time since we've owned Jack, I feel a connection to him. Perhaps we will become friends or at least cohabitants, residing together with a commonality joining us.

Billy takes Jack's leash and tries to lead him out of the room but Jack won't move. The dog just stands there staring at Billy. He doesn't like men. He just watched his mom get murdered by a man so I understand his hesitation about going with Billy. He doesn't like Billy, never has. Maybe his voice scares him. Who knows? Stupid dog!

"Maybe just pick him up if he won't follow you." I suggest.

Billy bends down, gently wrapping his arms around Jack and carefully lifts him off the ground. Jack spins his head around and bites Billy's arm, not hard enough to break the skin but frighteningly enough to make Billy quickly put him down. Billy's face turns red. He's either embarrassed or angry. They exchange glares and Billy's nostrils flare.

Dr. Messley comes to Billy's aide by checking out his bite wound. "Jack's been a little fussy around men." He looks up at Billy's face. "I think you'll be all right. He didn't puncture your skin. You're lucky. He could have done a lot more damage."

"I'll walk him out. Thanks Doc." I take Jack's lead from Billy who is more than willing to hand it over. Jack follows me while staring at Billy and threatens him with low growls to keep him at bay.

Jack, Billy and I leave the vet's with pills, cream and an appointment to return in two weeks to check his stitches. At least they won't have to remove them, since they're dissolvable. The ride back to Billy's is quiet, a few whimpers from the back seat when we bounce over unavoidable potholes in the road. I try to concentrate on the music that Billy put on to break the silence or perhaps to drown out the dog's cries. I try to sing along. I don't want to think about mom. It's just too painful.

We pull up in Billy's driveway and see that Deputy Walters is standing by his car, sipping on a glass of lemonade, talking to Billy's mom. He looks uncomfortable. He's so shy and awkward most of the time.

Billy opens the back door and stands off to the side so I can help Jack out of the car. I walk over to the deputy, dog in tow. "Hi, are you here to see me?" Jack growls at Deputy Walters then hides behind my legs.

The deputy shifts nervously as I approach. He sets his glass down on the hood of his car before picking up a stack of papers and handing them to me. "Is the dog going to be all right?"

I look down at Jack and nod. "Yeah, he'll be fine in a few weeks. I might change his name to Gimpy though."

"I don't think he'll mind." The deputy nods his head. He points at the papers that I now hold. "You said you wanted those. They're photocopies of each page in your mother's day planner." Deputy Walters says. When our eyes meet, he becomes a little flustered. He averts his eyes. "I took the book out of evidence to copy it. Of course, I can't just give you the actual book. You understand."

I flip through the stack for a moment wondering if evidence of blood on any of the original pages can be seen on the photocopies. I quickly shake the thought away and vow that if I see any, to pretend they're just smears of chocolate that was accidentally spilled on the original pages by my mother during her sweets attacks. Besides, the book was in her study, not her bedroom where she was murdered. There shouldn't be any blood on them.

"Thank you for getting this to me so quickly. I really appreciate it. I'll have to go through it and make a lot of calls. I'm not looking forward to it." I swallow the lump in my throat as I imagine the expressions on the faces of the people at the other end of the phone.

"You are very welcome. If you don't think you can make the calls, just make up a list and I'll take care of it for you. I don't mind." The deputy says as he shifts his feet and slides his hands into his pockets, shrugging his shoulders.

"Nah, I think I can handle it, but thanks anyway. I'll keep you in mind, though." I try to smile when he glances up at my face and wonder if it comes across looking as phony as I think it does.

I turn to walk away but only get a few feet before the deputy walks after me and calls to me.

"Katie, there's just one more thing." He says in nearly a whisper, "If you come across anything that looks suspicious, like information that your mother may have written in any of her notes... call me directly. It's just that I have a strong feeling that she discovered something that someone didn't want her to know and that's why she died."

Why does he need to point this out? "Of course." But I wonder why he would think that I wouldn't turn over any information that I might find especially if it meant finding her killer. And why should I call him directly? "Yeah, Sheriff Johnson already mentioned that."

"It's just that I can go over it right away and let you know if it's relevant. The sheriff might not have the time to dig into something that he feels isn't going to take him anywhere. He'd probably just hand if off to me to look into it anyway. That's why they have deputies, to do all the deciphering for them." He chuckles.

"All right, I'll keep that in mind." I nod at him.

"Okay, well I should get back. I'll touch base with you later to see how you're making out with your calls. I just want to make sure you're all right." He smiles, I shrug. The deputy thanks Billy's mom for the lemonade and climbs into his cruiser.

All I can do is stand there holding the stack of papers. His eyes hold mine for a moment and my stomach flutters. He starts the car and slowly drives off.

I hug the papers tightly as I slowly walk to the house, pulling Jack's leash forcing him to follow me. Since my hands are holding the papers, Billy's mom helps the ailing dog up the stairs and into the house. He doesn't flinch or try to bite her, even though he's never met her before.

After making him a soft bed to lie down on in the room where I sleep, he curls up and dozes off quickly. I sit at the kitchen table, phone in hand, and prepare to start calling people. I flip through page after page, not sure where to start. Who do I call first? Perhaps I should start with mom's agent.

I look through the list until I find Minnie Calverson. Minnie is the sweetest woman you'll ever meet, unless you piss her off. In that case, she can degrade and humiliate you with a look. Her words can permanently scar when she lashes out at you, but only if she feels that you purposely did her an injustice.

I love Minnie. She's as close as I've ever had to an aunt. My mother thought of her as a sister, a confidante, someone worth trusting. She's spent many vacation weeks here at our house. She and my mom would sit looking out over the lake for hours while they shared a bottle of wine. They would talk and laugh, sometimes even cry. She meant the world to my mother.

I quickly push her phone number into the keypad. The phone starts ringing and for a moment, I panic. I hadn't thought about what to say. How do I tell her that mom's dead?

This is going to be the worst news she's received since she got the call, four years ago, that her sister had died from lung cancer. I remember how my mom and her sat, crying, for hours before the funeral. My mom didn't leave her side through the whole dreadful experience. My mother was so strong for her. I envied her strength that day.

I clear my throat, swallowing a huge lump. Panic grips me the moment I hear her say, "Hello. Minnie Calverson. How can I help you?"

"Um, Minnie, it's Katie Mason here." I hesitate for a few seconds, just long enough for her to talk.

"Hi Katie. How are you? How's your mom? I've been meaning to call her but I got so caught up with work that I couldn't spare a moment. What's up? Is everything okay?"

I continue to say nothing. I know that in a moment from now, her life will fall apart. Like me, she will never be the same. I feel guilty for having to be the one to give her the news that will cut her so deeply.

"I have something to tell you." I take a calming breath hoping that my voice doesn't quit on me. "Mom... Mom was murdered."

Seconds pass with not even her breath being heard over the line. Then, "What?" she says in a shaky, meek voice.

"The night before last, someone came into the house and killed her. We don't know who did it. I found her in the morning... in her room. Minnie, I don't know what to do?" At this point, I fall apart. Tears pour from my eyes. A harsh groan escapes my throat. I hear her pain in her voice though she tries desperately to hide it... probably for my benefit.

"I'll be there as soon as I can. Don't you worry about a thing. I'll take care of everything once I get there. Don't make any other phone calls. I'll take care of all that too." She pauses, probably fighting back a scream.

I remember the shrills that came from me on that horrible morning but when I did, it sounded like it was someone else wailing the most pitiful, heartbreaking shrieks that I had ever heard. "Okay. I'm staying at Billy's for now, until they release the house back to me." I manage to say before another flood of painful tears spill from my swollen eyes.

"I'm going to hang up now. I want you to get some rest. I will be there as soon as I can." Minnie manages to say even though her voice is quivering and about to fail her.

I speak so softly that I'm barely audible, "Okay, I'll try." The click on the line lets me know that she's hung up. I can picture her screaming as the realization that her whole world is changing. Her best friend, and highest selling client, has been murdered and she has to find a way to live with the emptiness of her loss.

CHAPTER 8

Minnie arrives first thing in the morning and takes over the whole situation... just like my mother would have done. Her eyes, however, evidence her anguish by being so swollen and red. Her skin is pale, hair tangled. The sweatsuit she wears has coffee stains on the chest.

The moment she walks in the door and I get a good look at how disheveled she is, I erupt into a crying fit. Even though she's falling apart, she holds me until I cry myself into a deep sleep.

When I awake, Minnie isn't with me any longer. I can hear her in the Staples' den making funeral arrangements. Even though she's trying to keep her voice down, I can still hear the mournfulness in her words.

Minnie has decided to stay in a motel instead of at the Staple's house even though the offer was made. She comes to see me every chance she gets and is keeping me in the loop about funeral plans. She has made most of the hard decisions, which I will be forever grateful.

We don't have a day of visitation previous to the burial, so it's only a one day event. The funeral is quick, thankfully. We had a viewing in the early morning for only an hour then left to have lunch. At two o'clock we had another viewing with the funeral to immediately follow.

I think everyone in town has showed up to either pay their respects or just to get the latest gossip about what's happened. Most people are kind to me. Others just ignore me and I am fine with that.

Minnie got angry at a few of the teenagers and persuaded them to leave by humiliating them in front of everyone. They were disruptive and actually laughing at the back of the room. I didn't recognize them so I know they weren't there for any other reason than to have an excuse for leaving classes early today. It's not likely that my mother ever hung out with them or that they were here to mourn our loss.

While speeches are being delivered, I can hear sniffles coming from the people behind me. When I turned to see who's crying, I'm met by many red faces and weepy eyes all looking at me with saddened expressions.

My mother must have made a bigger impact on the people from our small town than I ever thought. Mom mostly kept to herself because she was shy. She didn't go out of her way to talk to a lot of people but could hold her own in a conversation when one was initiated. Maybe those attending are mostly fans of her writing. I don't recognize a lot of the faces.

The Staple family sits directly behind Minnie and me. Behind them are Carl and Rose Foster. In the next row back is Ben and Veronica. Behind them sits Jedd Harris, the town doctor, along with Henry and

Susan Wallace. Mr. and Mrs. Wallace were both great friends of my mother. Susan often brought fresh eggs and fruit from their small farm over to us. Henry tagged along most of the time.

I also see Hal Tessier, the town electrician and his family. He's worked on a few odd jobs at our house. He's a very nice man, quiet. My mom used to say that he wouldn't say boo to a goose if he had a mouthful... whatever that means.

Also attending is Timmy Baker. He's is the town plumber. He's 32 years old, single and speaks very loudly. He's the voice you'll hear above all others in a crowded room. He took over the plumbing business from his father when he retired two years ago. He seems nice but my mother didn't really like him. Perhaps his gruff manners scared her because of how abrupt my father used to be with her.

Somehow I managed to make it through the ceremony without losing my mind, screeching and dropping to the floor, covering my ears, rocking back and pretending it wasn't happening. I either clung to Minnie or Billy, rarely standing by myself.

Minnie is talking to the funeral director about the cremation that is to follow today's final good-bye and Billy is in the washroom. I find myself alone and vulnerable. I watch as Clete Perry weaves his way through the departing crowd to get to me.

Standing in front of me with his hat in his hand is an awkward middle-age man with short brown hair and brown eyes. He's tall - maybe 6'2" - and his shoulders are wider than anyone I have ever met.

"Katie, I'm really torn up by what's happened. Your mom was a wonderful person. I cared about her a great deal. I don't know if your mom ever said anything about me but I always wanted to court her. Of course she never accepted my affection."

109

"Um, no I never knew that." I'm not sure what to say to him. This is news to me. Why wouldn't my mother tell me that Clete was interested in her? Why wouldn't she go out with him? He seems like a really great guy: quiet, hard-working, an honest, caring type of person. He would have been perfect for her.

"She always said that she wanted to focus on you and her writing... that she didn't have the time to invest in a relationship. I kept asking though. I was hoping that maybe after you went off to college she might reconsider." Clete drops his head and wipes his runny nose with his crumpled tissue.

"Thanks for telling me, Clete. At least I know that she knew someone cared, other than me," I say without knowing if it's what he wants to hear. I can see the sorrow in his face as he fights not to give in to a tearful meltdown.

"I loved your mom very much. I know that she cared about me, too, but she just wasn't ready. I just want you to know that I do care a lot about you, as well, and if you ever need anything, I'll always be around. Just call me, okay?" He nods and quickly rushes out the door.

I drift off in a daydream about what it would have been like if they had started a relationship. What if he had moved in with us? Would we have lived at his house or ours? Would I have called him dad? Probably not. I wish my mother would have accepted him so that he'd have been here with her, protecting her. He's the type of guy who would have defended her with his life. She might still be alive.

Minnie shakes me to wake me from my thoughts. We leave the funeral home and drive to the cafe for coffee and a bite to eat while they cremate my mother's body. I try not to think about it but the unpleasant images burn through my brain. Every bite of my muffin sticks in my throat, stuck on the lump that I'm also trying to swallow. I cannot let go of my self-control. This is not the time, nor the place.

CHAPTER 9

My mother's ashes sit in a beautiful urn on the mantle above the fireplace. It's been three weeks now. Even though I've moved back into the house, it feels empty without her.

The house has been cleaned and all traces of blood have been removed. They tell me that my mother's room is mostly empty but I can't bring myself to open her door to see for myself.

It's always the same; I stand in front of the closed door and hesitate to touch even the handle. But when I finally talk myself into grasping it, my mind flashes images of my mother's corpse lying in her bed of blood.

In my imagination, I see her sit up. She looks at me with her arm stretched out toward me, begging for my help. Blood pours from her gaping neck wound just before her head falls backwards and hangs against her back, attached only by a few slivers of skin.

Back to reality, my heart is racing and I'm gasping for air. I yank my hand from the knob and rub it furiously on my shirt; as if it will somehow erase the ghastly image my mind has created. Maybe one day I will open that door, but for now, I will try to avoid it at all costs.

Minnie has left to return to her work. The agency has been, basically, at a standstill since I called to give her the news. Her secretary and her assistant have been trying to keep the business afloat but they can't do it forever. They need Minnie more than I do right now.

The cops have questioned just about everyone in town and also some of the returned truckers who regularly come through town. Nothing has come of it though. So far, there are no hard suspects. The detectives say that there hasn't been any

DNA evidence that can't be reasonably ruled out. I'm losing hope.

Jack lies at the other end of the sofa on the blanket that he claimed as his when he was a pup. It's plaid with blue and green stripes. His eyes remain open, staring at me. I wonder what he's thinking. We have become accustomed to one another, existing in the same space, reliant on one another's company.

Perhaps he too misses my mom. I have little doubt that he does. He scratches and cries outside her bedroom door sometimes. I don't know how to help him. I reach over and pet his head, to let him know that I don't hate him. He just huffs and groans before closing his eyes. Perhaps he's angry at me for not opening her door to let him inside. Maybe he still thinks that she's in there.

I have been floating through the past weeks in a dreamlike state, barely living by normal standards. Between school during the day and working at the cafe most evenings, I've been keeping busy.

The shushes and lulls that fill the air when I enter a room or crowd are becoming commonplace. At first it was hard to ignore but I'm getting pretty good at it now. I know people are uncomfortable around me. They never know what to say.

At least the dreadful smiles and head tilts have eased off. Some people still seem to be ignoring me, as though I don't exist. Perhaps that's easier for them than having to acknowledge me and my 'situation'. I actually prefer the invisibility. At least being inconspicuous again means that things are slowly starting to return to normal.

People talk in the cafe quietly amongst themselves and with my virtual invisibility, I can eavesdrop when I walk over to pour them more coffee or take their dishes away. Over the last few years I've overheard vast numbers of secrets; so many that I could write a book and destroy a lot of lives, marriages and careers. But I'm not the writer in the family, my mother was.

"Katie? Are you okay?" A strong male voice interrupts my train of thought.

I blink several times, trying to refocus. I must have been lost in a stare. I realizing that I've been leaning on the counter at the cafe with my head in my hand. I quickly survey the patrons to see if anyone has been trying to get my attention.

"Are you all right, honey?" Sheriff Percy Johnson is sitting on the barstool closest to me with a file in his hand. His eyes are locked on mine with a concerned look.

"Yes, thanks: I'm okay. I'm sorry, did you want coffee?" I shake off my daydream, pick up a mug and place it in front of him before he even responds. I'd be surprised if he said he doesn't.

Sheriff Johnson always drinks coffee, day or night. He's here in the morning when we open, stops in periodically throughout the day and he's usually here when we lock up at night. We are the only place in town to get a quick home-cooked meal, so most folks like to congregate here.

The sheriff nods his head while I fill his mug and place the cream pitcher in front of him. I place the coffee pot back on the warmer. Before I can turn around to ask the sheriff if there's any new evidence in my mom's case, I hear Carl Foster call out from the kitchen that an order is up.

I pick up both dinner plates and walk them over to table #6. Maple Willows and Anna Parlor instantly stop talking when I approach their table. I know they were just talking about me. It's so obvious by the guilty expressions on their faces.

For a moment, I consider spilling the burgers and fries into their laps then topping it off with ketchup. But I don't because I love my job here at the cafe and don't want to get fired.

Anna asks me in her, ever-so-phony voice, "So Katie, how is the investigation going? Have they found who did it yet?" She's so fake.

I really want to dump this plate on her. She doesn't even care about me or my mom because time and time again she's proven herself to be such a self-centered bitch. "Nothing new that I know of." I answer as briefly as I can.

"I wish they could find who did it. It must be driving you crazy... not knowing. I suppose they'll figure it out soon because they've dragged in just about every male in this town for questioning." Anna says.

I know she's trying to get me angry. I cannot give her the satisfaction. "The sheriff is only doing his job. Somebody knows something. It's just a matter of time before they catch him."

"Oh, I don't know about that. It's a known fact that hundreds of crimes from all over Canada and the United States that go unsolved every year." She flashes her crooked, wicked grin at me.

"Well, let's just hope this case isn't one of them." Maple says. She knows what Anna is doing and is trying to ease the situation. "Thousands of cases are solved every year. There's no reason to think that this one won't. I am really sorry that this happened to your mom... and to you."

I know that Maple is genuine because when you get her separated from Anna and that group of friends, she's really a nice person. She only hangs around that nasty group so she can benefit from their popularity. Even though her grades are near perfect, she can't become class president unless she has the support from her peers.

"Thanks Maple. It'll get solved. It's just taking longer than I'd hoped," I say to her then walk away before Anna has a chance to say anything else. I hear the two of them start to argue in whispering voices as Maple tries to defend me but I pretend that I hear nothing.

I return to the counter, grab the coffee pot and begin filling people's mugs. When I fill the sheriff's mug, he places a file on the counter between us. He opens it, revealing papers. I stand holding the pot as I look at the file.

"I wanted to talk to you about something. Now, you might not want to hear this but I've got to tell you." He sighs heavily before handing me an official looking paper. "Did you know about this?"

I read the note from the Correctional Service Canada. It's stating that my father is no longer a prisoner. He's been paroled. He's been out for nearly six months.

He can't be out! His sentence isn't up yet. The reason given for release is good behaviour and overcrowding? He murdered someone and he got out because of good behaviour? I don't think he even knows what good behaviour means let alone to do it. How is this possible?

Someone touches my shoulders. I jump. Ben Foster is holding onto me. "Are you all right? Katie, what's the matter? You're pale as a ghost."

"She'll be all right, Ben. Katie just got some bad news." Sheriff Johnson explains. "Now Katie, I can tell that you didn't know about this just by your reaction but I'd like you to give me a verbal yes or no. Did you know that your father was out of prison? And if so, did you voluntarily leave that information out of our investigation in order to protect him?"

I hand him back the paper with shaking hands. "No, I had no idea. How can he... How could they..." I have to hold my face with my left hand in order to stop my head from involuntarily shaking back and forth. "Why weren't we informed? What if he tries to find me? Wait, do you think he killed my mom?" My blood feels icy as it pumps through my veins and my eyes widen.

The realization that this might be the answer, hollows out my body. A sinking feeling fills the hole. Stars dance in my eyes. I blink and breathe deeply.

The sheriff takes the paper, slipping it back in his file folder. Without looking up at me, he explains, "Well now, they are supposed to inform the victims involved in the perpetrators crime or any witnesses that were threatened by the incarcerated person. When I asked them if they had contacted your mother, I was told that they couldn't find her. They said that she hadn't left any updated contact information."

I interrupt him, "Where is he now?" I grip the counter to help steady myself.

He raises sympathetic eyes to meet mine. "They don't know. He hasn't checked in with his parole officer in two months. There is a warrant out for his arrest. He'll have to go back to prison and serve out the rest of his time."

Ben drops his arms to his sides. He is now staring at the sheriff with his mouth wide open. He didn't know anything about my dad, nobody does. Mom and I vowed to keep it a secret from the folks in this small town. I haven't even told Billy the whole truth and he's my best friend.

I pick up the coffee pot from the counter and turn sharply to put it back on the warmer but my hand lets go. The pot crashes to the floor, glass scattering across the ceramic tiles. The sharp sound of the breaking glass sends the dreary patrons into a clapping frenzy.

It's common in this town for the diners to clap wildly when something gets broken. I don't know why, maybe to embarrass the person who dropped it so they will avoid it in the future.

They quickly stop clapping when they realize that this situation doesn't require any humiliation. I hear gasps and whispers but what throws me over the edge is the giggling that I hear coming from Anna.

Tears gush as an overwhelming panic rips through my brain. I clutch my chest and gasp for air. What if my father really did murder my mother? What if he came back for his revenge? My mother helped convict him. How did he find us?

When I attempt to pick up the broken glass, Ben once again grabs my shoulders. He holds them tightly and looks into my eyes. "Katie, you should just go home. I can handle it. It's not too busy today. You're of no use in the condition that you're in. Take the rest of the night off. Do you want me to call someone to come get you? You don't look very good."

Having felt the blood drain from my face, I must look pale as a ghost. I shake my head back and forth. Slowly I remove my apron and hand it to him before taking my purse and jacket out from under the counter. I'm not even thinking. It's like my body is moving on autopilot. I don't even ask the sheriff if he needs me for anything else. I just leave.

The tears drip heavily from my cheeks as my shaking fingers try to work the keys to unlock the car door. I sit behind the wheel of what once was my mother's car and sob.

A tap at my window makes me jump. Deputy Walters is looking at me, waving his hand, asking me to roll down my window.

"Are you all right, Katie?" He asks looking very concerned.

I shake my head while I wipe my face on my sleeve. "No, but I will be. I just found out that my father was released from prison and is on the lam. I'm just... I don't know."

"The sheriff called and told me but I couldn't get here before he told you. He probably wasn't very gentle in telling you either. He can be a bit harsh sometimes. Do you want to sit somewhere so we can talk about it? You shouldn't drive when you're this upset." The deputy asks.

"No, not right now, but thanks. I just have to get away from here. I need to be alone. I'll be fine and I will drive safely, I promise." I say as use my other sleeve to wipe away the remaining wetness on my chin.

"All right then. You take care, Katie. Call me if you want to talk about it." The deputy taps the roof of my car then walks toward the cafe.

I put up my window and start to drive. Before I even realize it, I've parked just off Lowell Lake Road by the falls. I take the keys out of the ignition and zip them up in my jacket pocket before stepping out of the car.

The trek down the steep jagged rocks is treacherous but I'm familiar with the easiest way down them. Billy and I come here a lot in the summer to sit in the river on the rocks and let the cool water splash against our backs, washing away the stresses of the day. I always feel refreshed when I leave here so maybe that's why my subconscious mind brought me here.

I perch upon a large boulder and watch the water pass below. Cupping my hands, I scoop the icy water and splash my face several times. Each time the water touches my skin I can't help but gasp. I wish it were summer again so I could slide in but the water is unbearably cold at this time of year.

I watch in envy as a crayfish moves its way between the rocks in the crystal clear water. I wish I were it, right now; free of all this stress. I want to go back to this morning when I woke up and didn't know about my father's freedom. Better yet, I'd like to go back to the evening before my mother was killed. Things would be very different today if I could have a redo, knowing what I know now.

My thoughts drift back to when the three of us lived together in that crappy apartment above the hardware store in our old town. My strongest memory of my father's brutality still plays out in nightmares from time to time. I was about seven years old. Dad and I were quietly sitting at the dinner table while mom served us. She put a piece of chicken down on my father's plate. His arm flew up, the back of his hand slapping her across her face. It happened so fast.

Mom fell backwards, hitting her head on the cupboard door. Blood oozed from her wound. He picked up his plate and threw it like a Frisbee at her face. It split the skin open under her left eye. She forever bore that scar.

My father wasn't quite satisfied just yet. He then grabbed that piece of chicken she had given him and shoved it in her mouth, forcing her to eat it, bones and all. He wanted a steak that night. I guess he thought she should have automatically known what he desired. I know that he hadn't told her because he was at his friend's house all day. I remember because the food sat in the oven waiting for him to get home. We never ate dinner without him, we weren't allowed to, no matter how hungry we were. But dad didn't need a legitimate reason to hurt my mom. Any passing excuse would do.

I can clearly recall what I was thinking right after it happened. I was angry at my dad for hurting her but also upset that my chicken ended up on the floor. I remember eating it anyway because I was so hungry. There were so many of those events that I can't recall them all.

I must have been sitting here by the river for quite some time; the dimness of the evening is taking over the daylight. A car pulls up on the cliff overhead, parking beside mine. "Katie, are you down here?" Billy's voice echoes off the rocks across the river.

"I'm here." I yell back to him. He makes his way down the embankment then sits on the rock next to me. He playfully bumps my shoulder with his. When I look up at him, he smiles, hoping I'll smile back but I just can't. Too many emotions are filling my head right now. A migraine is building and I'm exhausted from crying.

"I heard about what happened. Ben called me. He was worried about you. I'm sorry. I went to your house but you weren`t there so this was the only other place I could think of to come. Are you going to be all right?" Billy asks.

"Eventually, I hope." Now I make a pathetic attempt at a smile. "I'm just so angry. Why didn't my mother give the prison system our phone number? I mean, if she had, then maybe she'd still be alive."

"Wait a minute! First of all, she probably wanted to leave your old life behind. By how you've been so secretive about everything, it must have been pretty shitty. Second, how do you know that your father did it? I mean, there's no proof of that." He might be right.

I cut him off, raising my voice. "And we don't know that he didn't. It doesn't matter now anyway. It's not going to change anything. Mom will still be dead and whether dad killed her or not, he's still an asshole." I pull my legs up and rest my chin on my knees.

"Why didn't you tell me about your father? I'm supposed to be your best friend and you conveniently left out that you had a parent in prison. The rumor mill is flying around town as to what it was exactly that your father did to earn his place in captivity.

There are some pretty wild stories courtesy of the townsfolk's imaginations. I would like to hear the true story from you, if you want to tell me." Billy picks at a red leaf that he rescues from the water as it drifts past. He hands it to me as though it were a precious flower. "Here you are, my lady."

"Thank you. I'll treasure it always." I take the leaf and toss is over my shoulder.

"Don't say I never gave you anything." Billy chuckles.

"About my dad... well, it's a long story but I'll shorten up for you. He was very abusive to my mom, mentally and physically. On this one particular night, he beat her and left her bleeding on the floor and then went to his favorite pub. He usually did follow that routine. I suppose he hadn't released all of his anger on my mother so he took it out on some poor, innocent shmuck that just happened to get in my father's way. My dad killed him, beat him to death. So he went to prison. It's the best thing that could have ever happened for my mom and me. After the trial, we sold almost everything we owned, which wasn't much, and moved from town to town, trying to disappear. My mom took odd jobs here and there. That's when she decided to start writing. Our past seemed to follow us because someone always found out who we were and started the rumor-mill going. My dad's case was a big deal in such a small town so word spread to other towns and so on. When we moved here, far away from where we came, we purposely left out anything that had to do with our past involvement with him and omitted information on where we lived before. We simply wanted a clean start."

"I understand why you didn't want to tell anyone, but you could have told me. I would have tried my best to understand and I'd never, ever tell another soul. You do know that, right?" Billy says. "I love you. You're my best friend. I would do anything for you. I think I would curl up and die if you ever left me."

"I love you too. I'm sorry but I couldn't tell you even when I wanted to. You see, mom and I made a deal that we wouldn't utter a word about our past, that we would never again mention his name. We really like this town and didn't want my father's reputation to cause people to shun us. So I couldn't tell you. Please understand."

"I already said I do." He smiles at me with one of his gleaming grins. "I'm sorry you saw the abuse that your father inflicted on your mother. No child should have to witness anything like that. Oh now I get it, is this the reason why your mom didn't use her real name on her books?"

"Well, yes but also to keep the crazy fans at bay." I return a smile. "Some of those people are freaks! They scream and cry when they see her. Can you believe someone actually tried to rip out a chunk of her hair? Maybe they wanted to grow a replica of her using her DNA or make a voodoo doll to torture her. Who knows? There are some murder mystery fanatics out there that are completely wacky." I giggle for the first time in weeks.

Billy wraps his arm around me and kisses my forehead. "Okay, are you done pouting? I'm getting awfully hungry. We should go back to your place and eat something."

"Fine, but you're cooking." I stand up and pat his arm. "Hey, thanks."

"Don't thank me yet, you haven't tasted my cooking. Even my neighbor's dog won't eat it." Billy jokes then shoves me toward the water but pulls me back before I fall in. "Saved your life! You owe me again." He smiles.

I slap his arm playfully. "No, I mean thank you for always being so nice to me... for not judging me for what my dad's done."

"Never happen. I'll just mock you for the stupid shit you do all on your own." He jokes more.

CHAPTER 10

Kids are cruel. The whole school is buzzing with the news about my having a convict for a father. Everywhere I turn there are whispers and of course, laughter from the meaner kids in the school. Things were starting to get back to normal around here but now I've been thrown back into the spotlight. Is it ever going to stop?

I sign myself out at 11:30 when my lunch period starts. There's no way I can sit through fifty minutes of unsupervised heckling. I just can't bear being the center of everyone's conversations any longer; not today.

Because of that one horrific day, I've gone from being the person that nobody notices, to being on everyone's radar. I really miss being the invisible girl who easily wanders through life, unnoticed.

Instead of going home, I stop by the police station. Inside, Deputy Walters looks up from his computer. "Hi, Katie. Aren't you supposed to be in school?" He looks at his watch.

"Yeah but I couldn't... people are staring at me and I just couldn't... Can I talk to Sheriff Johnson?" I ask.

The deputy stands up and puts his hands in his pockets. Sometimes he seems so nervous and jittery around me. "Well, he's not in. There was a call about bear prints out on the Smitherton property. They probably just want it on record in case it comes back and they have to shoot it."

The Smithertons aren't the only people to call in bear evidence on their property this year. Several others also have. People think it's the same bear making his rounds in search of food. Property owners have to inform the authorities because it can put people in danger. Imagine what could happen if one night someone just opens their door to find a bear staring back at them. It does happen from time to time.

Shooting up into the air is always the first attempt at scaring away a persistent bear. But some of them do come back. Sometimes bears can lose their fear of humans. That's when they become a big threat. In those cases, the animal almost always ends up being shot and killed.

The deputy then asks, "Is there something I can do for you?"

"Um, yeah, okay. Maybe you can help me. Is there any way that I can get a copy of all the reports on my mother's murder? I have a feeling that you're going to say no, but..." I look into his eyes, pleading my case. "What if there's something in there that I'll think is odd but nobody else sees it? That simple little thing might help catch the guy. Please? I have to do something. I can't just sit and wait."

The deputy looks down at his computer as if deciding whether to get them for me or not. He shakes his head. "I can't give you that. There are details in those reports that you don't want to know. Please try to understand. The autopsy report alone... the in-depth description of the murder and rape; how she suffered before she died..." He strokes his chin then looks into my eyes with compassion. "Katie, you don't want to read about that. You'll never forget it even though you'll want to." His voice is filled with sorrow.

Maybe he's right. As it is, I will forever see the final result of the crime in my nightmares. Perhaps viewing autopsy photos would further tarnish any happy memories that I have of my mother.

I squeeze my eyes shut, hoping to erase the image of my mother's body lying on those blood soaked sheets, head nearly severed, finger missing. I rub my hands over my face before taking a deep breath and opening my eyes.

"Please. I can handle it. After what I've actually seen and what I've been told, reading the detailed evidence in the file can't possibly make things any worse. At least this way, I'll know what happened. And if we can catch..." I almost say, my father, "the guy, then maybe my nightmares will stop." I can't look up at him, I'm beginning to cry. I blink rapidly trying to make them re-absorb the tears and not allow them to trail down my cheeks. I need to appear strong right now. If I show weakness, he's more likely to refuse my request.

"I tell you what, you wait here and I'll call Sheriff Johnson. If he says that it's all right, I'll pick through the file and give you what I can. No autopsy photos. I draw the line there, you've seen enough." Even though he's agreed to help me, he's still somewhat resistant. He's only trying to shield me from more heartache.

Nobody knows very much about Deputy River Walters. He seemed to drift into this town a few years ago and into his job nearly unnoticed. That's not all that unusual though. A lot of folks around here have sketchy or secretive pasts. Even still, he fits right in with everyone in this town. Everyone likes him.

It's not clear where he came from or how he got this job but he is really good at it. Maybe that's why nobody ever asks him questions about his past.

That's one of the great things about small towns like this, people might gossip about one another but they never seem to ask you for the truth. Maybe that's because so many folks have moved here to escape whatever life they had somewhere else. As long as the new arrivals don't cause any grief in the town, nobody gives a damn.

All anyone knows is that he grew up in a small town in Vancouver, British Columbia. His parents passed away in a car wreck and he has no living family. He's a nice guy who's very quiet.

Several minutes later, Deputy Walters returns from down the hallway. "I just got off the phone with the sheriff. He says that I can give you some information but he wants to go through the file himself first. So when he's done with that, I'll bring it to you. Will you be home later?"

"I work until 5:30 but I'll be home right after that. I'll just be getting caught up on some of my school work. I've really been slacking off lately." I pause before saying, "Thank you, Deputy Walters. I really appreciate it."

CHAPTER 11

I drive down the street to the local grocery mart to pick up a few things before heading home. I have a craving for pasta tonight but need a few ingredients.

It takes me several minutes before I get out of the car. I flash back to a memory of the last time I was here; I had a list that my mother had given me. Shopping was easier then. She told me what to get and I'd get it. This is just one more reminder that I'm on my own now.

I pretend that I'm so engrossed in my grocery getting that I don't notice the other afternoon shoppers whispering to each other and pointing in my direction. I just go about picking things up, reading their labels and either throwing them in the cart or placing them back on the shelf.

Lesley Jones, the mart's owner interrupts me. "Katie, hi. How are you? Is

145

there anything I can help you with today?"
He stands beside my cart, with his hands
holding it, preventing me from moving
forward.

Lesley is a fat man with very little
hair and a jiggly chin. It's hard to look him
in the eye when he talks because my sights
keep getting drawn back to his flapping
chin-skin. It seems as if it's waving at you,
urging you to look at it.

"No, I'm fine. Thank you." I reply
while forcing myself to keep looking at his
eyes. I have to look down at the cart in
order to keep from eyeing his chin. I am so
weak.

"Are you doing okay? I don't mean
with shopping today... I just... we all worry
about how you're getting along. It must be
really difficult to just get through the
everyday chores when you don't really
know what you're doing because you've
never had to do any of it before." Lesley

shifts his feet and scratches his head nervously.

"I'm good. I'm getting along well enough. There's a lot to learn but I'm learning. I have plenty of offers if I need help. Despite what everyone seems to think, I'm not alone. You don't need to worry about me. I'll be okay." I smile at him as best I can in an attempt to cover up the loneliness that I do feel.

"Oh, okay. I... I just wanted to let you know that everyone in this town just wants the best for you. You might think that we're being nosy but it's not that way at all. We only worry." He shrugs.

I nod. "Then I suppose you can let everyone know that I'll be quite fine and not to worry so much. I want to find who did it, punish him then put it behind me. I simply want people to leave me alone and stop pitying me so much." I sound angry. "Sorry, it's not your fault. I know that you care, Mr. Jones. I'm doing considerably well, really I am. I have to get going now." I gesture toward his hands that are gripped on my cart.

His smile as he passes me with a pat on my shoulder. I want to scream at everyone in the store to leave me alone and mind their own business. I wish they'd stop staring at me.

I pay for my groceries without hearing a single word from the checkout clerk. She vigorously chews her gum as she looks up at me after swiping the barcode of each of my items. Thankfully, I only have enough to fill two bags so it doesn't take long.

My keys are in my jacket pocket so I have to set one bag down on the hood of the car to get at them. As soon as I pull the key from my pocket, the bag tips over, spilling its contents all over the ground. I want to scream in frustration.

I unlock the door and fling the one full bag of groceries onto the passenger seat then proceed to pick up everything that fell. I actually have to get on my hands and knees to reach for two oranges and a green pepper that have rolled under the car.

I stuff them in the bag, which is now ripped, when I see two legs approaching me. I look way up to see who it is but he's blocked out by the sun's glare behind him. My mind flashes to my dream, my nightmare. I can't see who it is because the light behind him is too bright, placing him in shadow.

I must have gasped or something because whoever it is has grabbed my arm and is helping me stand up. His voice shakes me from the terrified haze of my memory.

"Hey girl, are you going to be all right?" His voice is deep and shaky. He reeks of whiskey and cigarettes.

I pull my arm from him when I realize who the voice belongs to. His name is Ajax Richardson. He is the town drunk. This man wobbles around town, talking to himself if there is no one around for him to harass. He follows folks around, blabbing on about how the government is out to get us or some other idiotic, alcohol-induced topic of his choice. Most people do everything they can to avoid a confrontation but some men have punched him in the face for getting too aggressive.

"Get away from me. I'm fine." I say to him. I pick up my bag and pull open my car door.

"I was only trying to help. Piss on you then." He turns to walk away but spins back and holds onto my door so that I can't shut it. "I'm sorry. I didn't mean that. You should really work on being nicer to people. Look, I know what happened to your mom and I'm sorry. She seemed like a nice lady, even though she never gave me the time of day. I just wanted you to know that."

I yank my door and slam it. Unfortunately my window is open. "Thanks." I manage to say before turning the key and driving away, leaving him standing in the parking lot.

Then I think about it. Maybe I should talk to him. He knows everything there is to know about the people in this town. He might give me a lead about who could have killed my mom. People talk around him as if he isn't there, kind of like how they used to be with me. There's a lot of information that is spoken around the invisible people that does not fall on deaf ears.

I spin the car around and pull into the spot closest to where Ajax has wandered. I hop out and walk up to him. He watches me approach then cowers when I get too close to him. I back off a little so that he doesn't think that I'm going to hit him.

His expression is fearful, uncertain. I talk in a soft voice so I can ease his anxiety. "I'm trying to find any clue about who killed my mother. You know everything that goes on in this town: have you heard anything?" I pull on each finger nervously cracking my knuckles.

He slowly lowers his hands and stands straighter. He wobbles slightly before putting his hand on the wall for support. "I've heard a lot of rumors but they won't lead you anywhere. Rumors are rarely ever the truth." He coughs. "I don't know anything." He speaks evasively.

"I don't believe you. I think you know more than you're saying. Please. Please tell me what you know." I beg.

"All I can tell you is that you shouldn't believe everything people tell you. Sometimes there's more to the truth than what people are telling you and showing you." He wobbles again.

"I don't understand."

"Of course you don't. Nobody listens." His bloodshot eyes wander off toward the sky. "Look, don't trust anybody. Do you hear me? Nobody! Have you ever heard the saying, a wolf in sheep's clothing? Well, believe it. That's all I'm going to say." He makes the gesture of zipping his lips shut and stares at me with wide bloodshot eyes.

I stare at him, confused for a moment. "Do you know who killed her?"

He lifts his head up and looks down at me from his nose. He points to his tightly shut lips then shakes his head before wandering off through the parking lot.

I turn to go back to my car but stop abruptly by someone's belly. Timmy Baker, the town plumber is right in front of me.

"I saw that idiot talking to you. Is everything okay?" He asks.

"Yeah, I'm fine. He was babbling on about something. You know him, nothing ever makes any sense. He's just an old fool." For some reason, I feel like I shouldn't tell him anything that Ajax said.

"I wanted to make sure you're good." He says then pats my arm and walks into the hardware store.

I get back into my car and drive home thinking about what the town drunk had to say to me. Who was he referring to? Who shouldn't I trust? I wish he had told me more. What is he afraid of? Or better yet, who?

CHAPTER 12

I rush home then shove Jack outside to do his thing while I put the groceries away. After letting Jack back in and refilling his food dish and water bowl, I lock up then head into town to the cafe. Instead of sitting around at home, bored, I might as well eat a salad at work before my short shift starts. I did skip lunch today and my stomach is cursing me for it.

When I arrive, Rose asks if I wouldn't mind starting right away because she's feeling overwhelmed. Carl, her husband and the cafe's cook, has a migraine. She's been running the whole place all day by herself. She looks a little ragged. I wish she would have called me.

Of course I agree to help her out. I dress in my apron and pull my hair back in a tight bun before picking up the coffee pot and refilling some mugs.

There are only eleven people sitting around but they're a loud bunch, giggling and trying to talk over everyone else. I don't mind, it keeps me from drifting off into my own thoughts. Sometimes we all need a break from ourselves.

By five o'clock the place is packed with quite a few hungry townsfolk. I'm rushing to take orders and keep everyone tended to. I'm quickly tiring out.

I enter the kitchen and see Mr. Foster putting on his hairnet. He looks tired and paler than usual. He smiles at me before taking over the grill, relieving his haggard wife.

Mrs. Foster whispers something to him and he nods his head then kisses her on the cheek. She exchanges her grease splattered apron for a clean one. She sees me and says, "Mr. Foster says that he's feeling much better now. I'm just going to catch up on some of these dirty dishes before we run out of the plates we'll need to serve to our customers. I'll come help you out front as soon as I'm finished. How are you holding up?"

I look at my watch and realize that time has flown by and I only have half hour left of my shift. "Better now." I smile. "I'm glad I decided to come in early. I just wish you would have called to let me know that Mr. Foster wasn't feeling well. I would have come in a lot earlier."

"That's fine. I just thought that I could handle it until you got here. I had no idea we would be so busy. I'm going to start washing, unless you need me out front."

"No, I think I have it under control. Do you need me to stay longer tonight?" I ask her.

"It's starting to slow down. I should be all right without you. Besides, Veronica should be here soon and she can help out if I need her." Mrs. Foster turns and heads over to the mound of dirty dishes that has piled up and begins scrubbing away.

Veronica is the Fosters daughter. She's been away at college and hasn't returned home for at least five months. I wonder why she's is now. Maybe she's out of money and knows the only way she can cheat her parents out of some is to come home and kiss up to them.

I'm surprised to hear that she'll be here. She swore that once she left this small town, she was never coming back. She wants to be an actress but from what I've overheard others say, she isn't very good and would have to pay people to watch her act. I do wish her the best.

To my regret, Anna comes in with Maple in tow. They sit at the two-person table by the bay window at the front of the cafe. Anna fluffs her hair while admiring herself in the reflection from the window. Maple pretends not to notice.

I force myself to approach their table. Anna flips her hair as she spins her head to scowl at me. "Oh, you again."

"Yeah, imagine that. I do work here, after all. If you hate me that much, why don't you go somewhere else?" I stare right back at her. My patience has been worn thin today and Anna is already riding my last nerve.

"Right, well, we can't have everything, can we?" Anna smirks at me. "I'll have a diet pop and a Caesar salad."

I look at Maple, pencil poised. "Hi Maple. What can I get for you?"

"Hi Katie. I'll have the same." She smiles at me so I smile back before retreating to get their sodas.

As I walk away, I can hear Maple whispering to Anna, suggesting that she be nicer to me. But Anna just tells Maple to shut the hell up. I don't hear anything else after that.

I get their pops and deliver them without further conversation then walk around filling empty coffee mugs and glasses of pop or water.

The salad orders are up so I take them to their table and set Maple's down first.

Anna says, "So I started reading one of your mother's books and I got so bored in the first chapter that I had to put the book down before I fell asleep. I wonder if I can return it to the book store and get my money back."

She glares at me and her lips twist into a crooked grin. All I see is red. Anger envelops me, a fire rages in the pit of my stomach. Maple is saying something but I'm past the point of caring what anyone else has to say. I dump the plate of salad over Anna's head then grab her pop and pour that over her, as well, as if it were a salad dressing.

The fire within me subsides. A smile forms on my face, stretching ear to ear. I burst out laughing in what must sound like nothing short of the fit of an insane person's. I turn to walk away when I see Mrs. Foster coming out of the kitchen, wondering what all the hysterics are about.

Her eyes open wide as she sizes up the situation and realizes what I've done. I keep laughing and take off my apron, handing it to Mrs. Foster. I'm still laughing as I take my purse and walk out the front door.

Most of the people inside are just staring at me with gaping mouths while others stand and clap wildly. Mrs. Foster stands there with a concerned look upon her face. I think she's worried that I've completely lost my marbles. I will call her later to apologize and ask to keep my job. I wouldn't blame her if she fired me though.

The whole drive home, I keep re-running the event through my mind, bursting into crazy laughter again and again. I keep picturing Anna's horrified expression as the pop drenches her. I feel so relieved, so free. I bet she'll never be a bitch to me again, at least not while I'm handling her food.

CHAPTER 13

I stand before my mother's bedroom door, once again, unable to twist the knob. How am I going to be able to read through the police file and learn about more of the nitty-gritty details of her murder if I can't even open this damn door? I jump when something catches my eye. Jack is walking over to me slowly, head down, pouting or perhaps just scared.

I back away from her door to the other side of the hall and slide down the wall. Jack sits next to me, also looking at her door. "Jack, what are we going to do? I miss her so much. I wish she could tell us what to do. She would have enough courage to open this door. I'm not as strong as she was. Jack, I really wish you could talk because you could tell me who took her from us. I know it won't bring her back but it sure would be nice to find out why he did it."

He rests his scraggly-looking furry head on my thigh. His eyes reflect sadness and heartache when they look up at me. I wish they could tell the secrets trapped inside him. I pet him and realize just how dirty he is.

"Tonight, you get a bath." His ears jerk back and his eyes open wide before he scurries away, fearing that terrifying word.

I had started cooking before this failed attempt to open the door. I can hear the meat sauce bubbling on the stove so I head back in there to give it a stir and slip the noodles into the pot of boiling water.

Just then, the hair stands up on the back of my neck and an eerie coldness passes through me. The back wall of my house is made up of several large windows and a set of patio doors. I cannot see what resides outside those panes of glass. The pitch of night causes a mirror effect. My image reflects back at me. My heart races and all my instincts perk up. As though he feels it too, Jack whimpers and scurries to his pillow beside the sofa.

My eyes dart to the latch on the patio door; it isn't locked. I instantly regret that I left it unlocked after bringing Jack in after he peed on his favorite tree less than twenty minutes ago.

With my knees shaking and every fiber in my body telling me not to, I walk over to the sliding glass door. Each step closer brings a sharper fear that someone is going to slide it open and run in at me. I try to walk but the last few steps become a run. I lunge at the door and set the lock. My heart is pounding so hard that I can hear it in my ears.

For a few brief moments, I stare out into the darkness wondering if the murderer is watching me at this very moment. He could be a few meters away and I wouldn't be able to see him. All I can see is a blurry image of myself, staring back at me. The moon is but a sliver and not casting any glow. I step closer to the glass, my nose nearly touching. I cup my hands around my eyes to block out the inside light, desperately trying to make out any forms resembling a human but my breath just fogs up the window, obscuring my view.

I shake my head trying to convince myself that I'm just overreacting. With my eyes closed tightly, I take a deep breath then exhale slowly. I turn and head back to the kitchen.

I stir the sauce and notice the fog from my breath seems to be lingering on the glass door. I've never seen the steam from my breath linger so long but I shrug it off.

The doorbell chimes making me screech, tossing the ladle up in the air, only to land halfway across the kitchen. Pasta sauce is now spattered on the ceiling, counter, floor and my shirt. I groan in frustration before I find out who pushed the bell.

I have to shush Jack from barking. I think he jumped higher than I did when the bell sounded. "Jack! Shut up!" He quiets to a low growl and scurries along beside me as I make my way to the door. He hides behind my legs. He's such a coward!

My heart pounds as I gather the courage to pull the curtains aside and look through the window to see who is standing on the other side of the door. Could it be the killer? Will I see a pair of wild eyes glaring back at me? Why would a crazed killer ring the doorbell? Would he not just break in? I squeeze my eyes shut again, hoping to conquer my wild imagination.

I move the curtain to see who it is. Deputy Walters sees me peer out and holds up a file. I open the door and invite him in. He walks in and glances around while I shut the door and lock it. Relief calms my temporary insanity because nothing can keep me safer than having a man of the law here.

Jack sniffs the deputy's leg but when Walters bends down to pet the dog, Jack's paws frantically claw at the floor, fighting to gain traction. He beelines it to his bed and continues to emit low growls. I think he's trying to keep the man at bay with what he thinks are terrifying sounds. I roll my eyes.

"Don't mind him. He has this issue with men, some more than others. I don't know why. He'll shut up eventually." I try to apologize for the dog's actions.

"It's not a problem. He's been through a lot." River smiles at the dog then looks back at me. "I brought the file. There's a lot of stuff blocked out because we can't legally give you that information since it is an ongoing investigation. I'm sure you understand." He hands me the file.

"No, I don't really understand. I mean, it's MY mother's murder. Shouldn't I be privy to all the information?" I toss the file on the kitchen table. "Come on in. Make yourself at home."

He removes his shoes and follows me to the kitchen. His eyes automatically seek out my mother's bedroom door, the scene of the crime. I can see the expression on his face change. He notices me looking and tries to smile to cover it up but it's not a very convincing smile, so he stops.

"How are you doing? You know, being back here after..." He pauses and looks back at that closed bedroom door. "Are you okay with living here?"

"No, I'm not. I hate looking at that door and not being able to open it. I have nightmares every night that someone is watching me. But, this is my home. Where else am I going to go?" I start wiping up the mess on the counter.

"I'm sorry. The last thing I want to do is upset you. I... I'm just concerned. You can always sell this house and find another. You don't have to stay here." He's trying to help.

"Deputy Walters, my mother loved this house. She put her heart and soul into it. This was her sanctuary from the lingering terrors from her past. She felt safe here. Isn't that ironic?" I say, with a hint of cynicism while I climb on the counter and wipe the sauce off the ceiling.

He notices the splatter and asks, "Should I ask? Not that anyone would do it but I've heard that if you toss spaghetti on the wall and it sticks, it's done. But, I don't think it applies to the sauce." He laughs.

"Ha ha, you're very funny. The doorbell... I wasn't expecting it." I giggle when I think about how stupid I must look to him right now.

"Please, just call me River. Deputy Walters just seems so formal. When you're done with that, I'd like to go over the file with you in case you have any questions.

But I see that you're about to eat dinner so I can come back another time." He turns to leave.

"I made enough for two. I'm still not used to cooking for just one person. Mom always let me make dinner because I love cooking, even though I'm not very good at it. Would you like to stay? I could use the company." I hate feeling this lonely. I miss having my mom here.

"Are you sure? I don't want to impose." River shifts from foot to foot nervously.

I climb off the counter then take out two plates, placing them on the counter beside the stove. "Please stay. I insist. After dinner, we can review the file." I slide the salt and pepper over to him and gesture for him to put them on the table. I was just going to eat over the sink but since I have a guest, he might appreciate using the table.

Throughout dinner, I find myself staring at the file and not being a good hostess by holding up my end of the conversation. He seems to understand so we eat dinner in silence. The only thing he says is that the spaghetti tastes delicious and that he hasn't had a home cooked meal in a very long time.

While the dishes are soaking in the sink and we've flipped through the first few pages in the file, I come across a page about DNA swab results.

"Why are the names of the people blacked out?" I ask.

"You have to remember that it's an ongoing investigation so we have to black out some things that you're not supposed to see, such as the names of the possible suspects. The last thing the case needs is you stalking the people on this list and accusing them of committing murder. Not that I think you'd do that but it would taint the case if you did." His face is expressionless; I can't tell what he's thinking.

"So how am I supposed to give you any information about how a specific person's DNA got into my mother's room if you don't tell me who's DNA you found? My input on this could be relevant to solving the case. If you help me, I'll help you." I'm trying not to get upset.

He pulls the file over so it's in front of him. "I tell you what, if I were to ask you about certain people, not necessarily any of these suspects," he points to the chart, "could you tell me what you know about them?" He looks at me with a conspiring expression.

He's going to give me their names. I nod my head anxiously. I curl my leg up under me so I can lean in closer to the file in front of him. I want an unobstructed view.

He points to a spot on the report about a fingerprint found on my mother's bedpost. "Could you give me any reason why Clete Perry's fingerprints would be in your mother's room? More specifically, on her bedpost."

I huff, slightly disappointed. "He helps us out with moving heavy stuff sometimes. He's been in the house before, several times. Mom moved her bedroom furniture around about a week before..." My voice cuts off. I clear my throat then continue. "Clete moved her bed because it's solid oak and way too heavy for just mom and me to move. The print is legit. You can scratch him off as a suspect. Besides, he's been nothing but nice to us. He would never hurt my mom. He, um... he really liked her. He mentioned that at her funeral. I don't know why my mom kept that from me."

"I wasn't sure if you knew. He disclosed his feelings for her during his interview. He told us that he did care for her very much." River takes a few notes in his notepad before returning his focus back to the report.

His finger finds another blacked out section. "Has Ben Foster ever been in your mother's bedroom?"

"Ben Foster? No, not that I know of. You found his DNA in there?" My heart pounds wondering if there's any way that the gentle Ben that I know could even kill a fly, let alone commit such a horrific crime. "Where was it found?"

"His DNA matched a swab taken from a book on your mother's dresser. It was her book, one she wrote." He says.

Disappointment, yet again. "Oh, yeah that can be explained. He bought that book at a store when he was away at school so he gave it to me and asked if I could get her to sign it for him. I handed it to her a few days before she died. She had set it down on her dresser. I guess she forgot to sign it and give it back to me."

"I don't recall it being signed." He clears his throat. "Can you explain why Billy's hair was found in your mother's room? Has he ever been in there?"

"Um, I don't know. I don't think so but it's possible. I mean, he's here a lot. He's my best friend. I don't know why he would have been in her room though. I can ask him."

"No need. We already asked him and he says that he has no idea. It was probably just transferred to her bedspread from her nightgown. She could have picked it up from anywhere in the house and it just happened to drop there. You two are really close?" He forms it as a question.

I shrug my shoulders. "Yeah, Billy's my best friend, like I said. Ever since I moved here he's been there to protect me. He'd never hurt me or my mom, not ever."

"You're certain of that?" River asks.

"Yes, very. Do you doubt me?" I'm slightly irritated.

"No, I just want to make sure. Sometimes we think we know someone but we really don't. I'm just asking. Don't take it the wrong way." With his green eyes locked on mine, he smiles at me then runs his fingers through his blond hair.

He shifts his eyes nervously back to the file. "There's a fingerprint that couldn't be matched up to anyone in the database. It was found on the glass door at the back of the house. Whoever it belongs to doesn't have a criminal record."

I think for a minute before I remember how it could have gotten there. "Oh, now I remember. I told you guys about him. Some guy just showed up at the backdoor asking to use the phone. My mom told me that he was a truck driver and he said he had broken down. He also told her that his communication devices wouldn't work. My mom said that she didn't let him

177

in but did call a tow truck for him. I wasn't home. I was told about it after the fact."

"Yes, I remember you telling us about the mysterious truck driver. Do you have any idea why he went to your back door, not the front of the house?" He asks me.

"Mom told me that he said he rang the bell but nobody answered so he came around the back. She was just getting out of the shower and she probably didn't hear the doorbell." I wonder if it could have been that strange man who came back a week later and killed my mom. But why? Why would he do that after she'd helped him?

"A truck driver. It's a long way from the highway to this house. Why would he come here? Why not just follow the road? I know it's a longer walk but it would have led him to civilization." River thinks out loud. "He is now the biggest question mark in this investigation. We're looking into finding out who this guy is, exactly what he was doing here and why. You've helped by giving us somewhere to start searching for the person who belongs to this print. I'll look into towing companies to see who it was that helped out this truck driver so we can track him down."

"I wouldn't read too much into it if I were you. We have had a few travelers knock on our door at all hours of the day and night because their vehicles had broken down. It's not uncommon. Cell phones don't always work out here, not with the mountains blocking their signals. If you happen to be unfortunate enough to stall in a gully, you're going to be walking. Our lights are the only evidence of civilization from certain points on the highway and if you're going by a map, it looks like a really long walk to the town." I say, feeling slightly disappointed in the evidence because I doubt a lone driver did this. There's no solid reason as to why he would... unless he's a psychopath. They don't need a reason.

Deputy Walters leaves after reviewing the rest of the file with me. I'm feeling a little more relieved that her murder might not have been my father's doing after all. There's not one shred of evidence pointing to him. It's possible that the truck driver could have come back to murder my mom. It's a long shot, but I'll take it.

CHAPTER 14

School feels like such a waste of time. If I didn't need these two credits for college, I'd just quit all together. I'm really getting tired of my rude classmates. I'm trying every other second of the day not to remember that my mother was murdered but how can I when I'm constantly being reminded by my fellow students?

When I walk into class, Mr. Jacobs pulls me aside and quietly says, "So, Katie, I hear there was an episode with Anna last night at the cafe. Don't look so surprised. I'm sure the whole town knew about it within minutes of its happening. Nothing can be kept a secret in this town. You should know that by now."

"Ah, yeah. I'm sure it wasn't nearly as dramatic as everyone says. They've probably blown way out of proportion," I say, slightly embarrassed by my immature behaviour.

He chuckles. "Well, what I'm wondering is if there's going to be any issue with you two in my class today. You and Anna have to sit near each other: can you keep it together long enough to get through this period without incident?"

"For sure! I'll be fine as long as she keeps her eyes off me and doesn't say anything bad about my mother ever again. Otherwise, I can't promise anything." I smile at him.

He shakes his head. "All right, I'll talk to her and warn her that she'd best keep herself in check." He looks around to make sure nobody can hear. "I would have paid to see you dump that pop over her head. But I'll deny it if you tell anyone I said that." He gives me a mock-stern look.

I giggle again. "It was something else. I can't remember the last time I laughed that hard. It felt like all my troubles were washed away, like her make-up did when the pop ran down her face." I stifle a laugh as I walk to my desk at the back of the classroom.

Anna walks into the room with her nose in the air in her usual snooty way. Mr. Jacobs calls her over to his desk. He talks to her quietly as she stands, without saying a word, nodding her head and pursing her lips. She quickly slinks to her desk, her eyes looking down at the floor.

The class whispers and stares as she takes her books out of her bag, not acknowledging anyone. Even though I fight not to, I chuckle as I picture last night's event and that surprised look on her face. I do feel a little bad that she's so humiliated over it but only a teeny bit. She totally deserved it.

After class I make my way to my locker to put my books away and get my purse and keys so I can head home. I close the locker door and jump when I see Anna's face sulking at me from behind the door.

"I shouldn't have said what I said last night. I lied anyway. Your mom's book was really good. I finished reading it in only two days. I couldn't put it down." She looks everywhere except at me.

"So why did you say that?" I ask.

"I don't know. It's no secret that I don't like you, Katie. You aren't one of us. I mean, you're nice and all, but you're weird."

"If this is your way of apologizing, it sucks." I say as I turn to walk away.

"Wait!" She calls out to me so I turn back. "I'm sorry. Look, I'll never say anything like that again. I think I would lose my mind if someone killed my mother and I didn't know who did it. You are a lot stronger than I thought you were. I'll give you credit for that." She crosses her arms over her chest.

"Gee, thanks." I say as I wonder where she's going with this.

"This is a small town and we're going to have to deal with each other from time to time, so do you think we can just move past this? I don't mean that I want to kiss and make up but we should at least try to be civil." Anna says.

"Yeah, I can be social as long as you keep your snarky comments to yourself and behave like a normal, mature person." I reply.

"Okay, fine. I'll work at it." She says.

"You do realize nobody is going to let us live this down for a least a week, right?" I add as a smile creeps up on my face.

She smiles back but rolls her eyes. "I know. This is the most exciting thing to happened around here in a while. So shall we call ourselves frienemies?"

"Friends that are enemies? Yeah, sounds good." I nod with a smile then take my leave. It's homeward bound for me.

CHAPTER 15

I don't work tonight so this is a good opportunity to start looking through all the Halloween decorations. Mom stores all the Christmas, Halloween and Thanksgiving stuff in the dusty, cobweb-ridden attic. I could never figure out why she bothered to decorate when we live way out here. It's not like anyone is going to see them. But I think she put them up more for her benefit than anyone else. So I'll decorate... for her.

Jack follows me up the stairs into the attic. He's been glued to me for weeks now. He stares into each box as I open it, curious to smell what's inside. One by one I cut the tape and flip the tops to reveal more scary goblins and witches, lights and black candles. Until the second last box...

Unlike the others, this one is not taped shut. Hidden under two cardboard cut-outs of witches is something that doesn't relate to any holiday, even though it's labelled with the word "Halloween" written in black marker on the box top.

My mother was meticulous when it came to organizing, so this can't be a mistake. But why would she feel the need to hide newspaper clippings and notebooks in the attic? What was she working on that was so secret that she had to hide it up here and not just keep it in her office? Was she hiding it from me? It's not like I would have ever gone through her stuff. I never had an interest in her research when she was alive.

She didn't write non-fiction. Nothing was ever true to life. She did do a lot of research before starting to write a new novel because she would use real murder cases as a guide in her fiction. She never uncovered anything that required this much secrecy. Why would she hide this from everyone, from me? Who did she think would snoop through her things looking for it?

I pick up the box and carry it downstairs, abandoning the Halloween decorations altogether. I set the box down on the kitchen table and pull out the first article. I read aloud the parts highlighted in yellow marker.

June 7, 2007

Victoria, British Columbia

The body of a 12 year old girl was found mutilated just off a trail in Beacon Hill Park. Jennifer Michelle Presley had been missing for weeks. Her remains were found by a jogger. Her body was not concealed in any way.

The article goes on to say where she was last seen and despite how enormous the search parties were, they couldn't find her. That park had been scoured but after finding nothing, they moved on to other locations.

The detectives believe that she had been placed there shortly after her death, about a week before she was found. So whoever had her, kept her alive for seven days before finally ending her life.

I lay the article down on the table then take the next clipping from the box and read it.

April 21, 2007

Victoria, British Columbia

The remains of 11 year old Ashley Vanessa Hickles were found nude in Beacon Hill Park last night by a dog walker. A black Labrador sniffed out the remains which were hidden behind some brush and partially concealed under a pile of leaves.

Vanessa had been missing for 8 days. Her body had been dumped post mortem. It is estimated that she died only a few days before her remains were discovered.

The next article reads:

September 12, 2007

Victoria, British Columbia

14 year old Lucy Janice Beflore's body has been discovered hidden under a pile of brush. She was beaten and strangled causing her death approximately a week before being found by a search team.

There seems to be a pattern here. My mother was investigating a serial killer. But why? Was it for a book she was going to write? If so, why did she feel a need to hide all this stuff in a box under Halloween decorations? What did she stumble upon? Could this have something to do with her murder?

The next few articles are about serial killers and how detectives study the remains of the victims to learn the perpetrator's M.O. They can create a profile of this person in hoping that it will help to find him or her.

One of the articles describes how three more bodies of young girls have been found in various degrees of decomposition throughout Beacon Hill Park. The searchers continue to examine the area to ensure they have found all the bodies left by this serial killer.

That leaves a total of six bodies of young girls left to rot in Beacon Hill Park, in British Columbia. Why was my mother keeping articles about these murders stored away in the attic? I wonder how long they have been up here.

Two notebooks lie under more printouts of articles about serial killers and the searches implemented to track down him or her. I open the first one and scan through my mother's notes. She references the investigators that are working on this case.

What did my mother get herself into? Could this be why she was murdered? Is the serial killer living in our town? By reading this am I putting myself in danger as well? I will have to watch my back, just in case.

I walk away from the box and fill the kettle so I can make myself a cup of peppermint tea. I notice my hands are shaking. As the water boils, I stare at the box and the papers strewn about it. So many thoughts are running through my head. The main one being; I can't figure this out by myself. I need help.

I take my cell phone out of my pocket and consider calling the sheriff or the deputy but worry that this might not be anything more than my imagination running away with me. There may be other boxes, secretly stored away, that contain other researched cases and I just haven't found them yet. Or she simply made a mistake when she packed this box. It's not likely considering how particular my mother was at keeping everything in order.

But seriously, why would a serial killer hunt down my mother? First of all, he only kills little girls. Second, I doubt seriously that my mother learned who he was if the trained, seasoned detectives couldn't figure it out. My mom was a great researcher but I don't think she was able to unearth the truth that so many others couldn't.

I decide to call Billy instead. "Hi, what are you doing?"

"Hey girl, what's up? Nothing. I'm just sitting here studying for my biology exam tomorrow. I think I know everything I need to. What are you doing?" Billy asks.

I pause for a moment wondering if I'm being ridiculous. "I found a box that my mother was hiding in the attic. There were printouts of articles from British Columbia about a serial killer. It sounds crazy, I know, but I'm wondering if somehow this has something to do with her murder."

I can hear Billy breathing on the other end of the line for several seconds before he speaks. "I'm sure it's nothing. It's probably just some old research that she did for one of her books. She most likely put it in the attic to make more room in her office, not to hide it."

"Do you think I should hand it over to the sheriff? It's probably nothing but..." I ask.

"I wouldn't, not yet anyway. I'd want to go through it and see what it's all about before I handed it over to them. They'll probably just put it up on a shelf somewhere until they can get to it, whenever that might be. We should go through it first." Billy states. "Do you want me to come over?"

"No, not if you have to study. I don't want you to fail because of my overactive imagination." I insist.

"I'll be there in a few minutes." Billy chuckles then hangs up the phone.

Just then someone knocks on the sliding glass door at the back of the house. I nearly jump out of my skin. It slides open and Clete Perry sticks his head inside.

"I'm sorry, Katie. I didn't mean to scare you. How are you holding up?" He asks me.

"Um, yeah, I'm all right. I didn't hear you drive up." I take several deep breaths to calm my anxious nerves. "You scared me. I wasn't expecting anyone to knock on the door. How are you?" I ask him.

Clete pulls off his knit toque as he steps in the door, sliding it closed behind him. "Oh, I'm doing just fine. I really do miss seeing your mom around. How are you doing with all that?"

I do my best to smile at him convincingly, and then say, "I'm getting by. It's just hard sometimes. I dream of her from time to time. That makes me happy. Yeah, I'm okay."

He nods while he fusses with his hat. Jack slinks up next to Clete's leg and smells his boots. His tail wags only a few swipes. When the dog looks up at Clete, he leans down and pats his head. He says to the dog, "And how are you Jack?"

Jack wags his tail lazily then walks back to his bed and does a few circles before lying down. Clete is the only male that Jack has ever liked. That always baffled mom and me. He hates every man he's ever met, except Clete.

Mom and I used to make jokes that if it weren't for Clete's size, we may have thought he was secretly female. But, after closer observation, there's no way he's a woman in drag. He's a really goodhearted man so maybe that's what Jack sees in him.

"Well that's good then. If you ever need anything..." He pauses. "you have my phone number, so call. I've never been much of a talker but I'm a great listener."

"Thank you, Clete. I do have your number. What brings you out today?" I ask him, trying to change the subject.

"Oh yeah, I brought the cord of wood for your fireplace. There should be enough there to get you through the winter. If not I can bring some more. I'm going to stack it up on the side of the house for you." Clete says.

"That's fantastic. I was going to call you to ask you for more because the stack is getting pretty low. It just kept slipping my mind. But yeah, stacking it there would be great. Thank you."

"Sure, no problem." Clete shuffles his feet anxiously. "The police questioned me for several hours last week. It was awful. I kept wondering why they were investigating me when the killer is out there somewhere getting away with murder, literally. It makes me so angry."

For a moment, the image of Clete on top of my mother, slitting her throat, fills my thoughts. I quickly shake them away.

"They're trying to be thorough. I'm sure they've questioned almost everyone in this town. Don't take it personally. I know that there's no way you could have ever hurt my mom."

"I go to bed angry, have nightmares all night, and get up in the morning just as angry. They have to catch this guy. I need to know why he would take such a beautiful, gentle person away from us." He pauses. "I don't know why I told you that. You have your own pain to deal with and don't need to hear about mine. I'm sorry."

"I'm angry too," I say. "It's nice to know that I'm not the only one."

Clete nods. He pulls his toque back on his head, tucking his thinning brown hair up into it. "Well... call me if you need anything."

"Yes, of course. Thank you for the wood." I say as he nods once again before disappearing out the door and around the corner of the house.

CHAPTER 16

After reading through the clippings, printouts and some of my mother's notes, Billy and I are no further into discovering what it was that my mother was so desperate to hide.

She left long dashes where the suspected serial killers names should be, say, if the cops interviewed someone, she left that person's name out of her notes. So matching names of people to certain actions noted, and who are coincidentally living in this town, to the coded writings my mother used to keep her notes, will be nearly impossible for us. I don't understand the symbols and code my mother sometimes wrote with.

When tears start to fall, Billy wraps his arms around me. "Do you want me to spend the night? I can hold you while you sleep. I'll keep you safe so you can finally have a good night. Not to be mean or anything, but you look like shit. Personally I don't care because I always think you're beautiful. We should be a couple, you know. We'd make a good pair."

Through my tears, I laugh. "You know it would never work out; we're too close friends. You know that I don't see you in that way. But, thanks for the offer, again." I chuckle. "I'll be all right. Thanks for helping me with this. You need to go home and study for your exam. We're obviously not getting anywhere here. I think it's her research from something she was going to write about and decided not to. She would lose interest in some of the ideas she considered for possible novels. Maybe that's why it was in the attic. I'm sure it doesn't have anything to do with her death. It was just odd that she put it in the attic not labeled correctly. That's just not like my mother."

"Don't you have an exam tomorrow too?" Billy asks as he starts walking toward the door. "Put that box away and go study for it. I'll come back tomorrow so we can look through it after school."

"I'll do fine. It's only an English exam and I'm ready for it. You're probably right though, maybe I will just put everything away and go through the rest of it another day. I don't think it's relevant to her death."

"You do that, I insist. I can always take it home with me and go through it myself. I'll let you know if anything adds up. But, for you, no more tonight, okay? Promise me." Billy holds my chin, staring into my eyes. After I nod, he places a quick kiss on my lips. He's never kissed my lips before. It's always my forehead. He stares deeply into my eyes again but I look away, freeing my chin from his grasp. I stare at the floor and shuffle my feet.

"Well, yeah, sure...You're right, I should just wait until tomorrow when I'm not so exhausted. I can't make sense of anything tonight. But, I'll hang onto this stuff. My mom's hands wrote those notes and whether the words have any importance or not, the fact that she wrote in these books means everything to me. I don't want to part with them. I'm sure you understand. But thanks for the offer."

He nods his head and fakes a smile. "I understand." He slides on his coat without another word then heads out to his car.

After Billy drives away, I'm left wondering why he would kiss my lips. Does he truly want more out of our friendship? I shake my head, dismissing the thought. He's like a brother to me. It wouldn't be right.

I pull the last notebook out of the box before placing everything back in it. I put the box in my mother's office and the unread notebook in the drawer under the coffee table. We didn't get a chance to look through this one yet and I don't want to get it mixed up with the ones that we have.

"Jack. Jack, where are you?" When he doesn't come, I go in search of him. I find him upstairs in my room, hiding under my bed. He's never liked Billy. I don't know why, he just doesn't. Maybe it's because Billy's voice is really deep and he's just used to hearing mine and my mother's voices. Billy is male after all.

Mom and I have always thought that since Jack was a rescue dog, maybe he was abused by a man and that's why he's now nervous around them.

"Come on, scaredy-cat. He's gone. It's just you and me again." Jack's been especially terrified of men ever since my mother's murder. "Don't you want to go outside?"

His ears perk at the word 'outside'. He crawls out then slinks through the house, nervously scouting for Billy as he makes his way to the patio doors. After letting him out, I tidy up the dishes then let him in and get ready for bed.

My dream is filled with chaos, murder and blood... lots of blood. I dream of the dead girls in the newspaper cut-outs. It's so real that I can't tell if it's a dream or not.

In my dream, someone is standing at my door, watching me sleep. I flash to my mother, lying in gooey redness, a man standing over her massacred body. I struggle to see his face. Then I see that my mother's body has transformed into a little girl.

My throat is so dry. I try to scream but nothing comes out. I try to run but my feet are swallowed by a puddle of coagulated blood. He's getting closer to me. The knife in his hand is dripping with my mother's blood. Panic takes over every cell in my body. With great effort, I howl out the most bloodcurdling scream to ever escape my lungs.

Jumping out of bed with sweat dripping down my face, I wake to a quiet, empty house; no man, no blood, and my mother still dead. I sit quietly on the bed, tears pouring down my face, trying to calm my breathing, while I attempt to ease the fear that's taken over Jack. I must have nearly scared the death into him. For this quivering dog that I once couldn't stand, I now have pity.

It's only 6 o'clock in the morning. I don't have to get up for another hour yet. My head is pounding loudly. I can hear it in my ears. I take two acetaminophen tablets to ease the sharp, thudding jabs in my brain. I think a migraine is in the works.

I go downstairs and fill the kettle to make myself a tea. There's no chance of falling back asleep so I might as well start my day. The brighter side of waking up so early is that I'll be able to watch the sun rise up over the mountain.

Jack reluctantly goes outside to relieve his bladder. It's cold and he hates walking on the frozen dew that rests upon the blades of crisp grass.

I stare at the closed door separating me from the nightmare in my mother's bedroom. Open the door, I tell myself, but when I touch the handle and attempt to turn it, a flash of her nearly decapitated body overpowers my thoughts.

I gasp loudly and shake my head, in an attempt to rid my mind of the image. I turn to once again walk away defeated when something inside me spins me around.

As though operating under its own command, my hand has opened the door. It swings slowly with a creak that's so familiar to me. It's the sound I used to hear when I was stumbling around in the kitchen making breakfast. It reminds me of my mother opening her door to a brand new day.

I smile with my eyes closed, remembering how I would feel when she'd come around the corner into the kitchen, saying good morning to me. I took every day for granted. If I could go back in time, I would hug her forever.

I take a moment to build enough courage to open my eyes to whatever I'll see in that bedroom. I exhale quickly, relieved to see nothing but an empty room. I mean there's absolutely nothing in here; no carpet, no drywall, and thankfully no bloody body.

Everything is gone. I have to fix this room. It should be put back to the way it used to look. At the very least, it should have walls. My mother would want that. I'll call Clete Perry later today to see if he'd be interested in helping me out. He said to call him if I needed anything. He used to help mom with all kinds of things. I guess you could say he's our handyman.

I sit with my eggs, apple and hot tea at the kitchen table, Jack at my feet. I flip open the cover of the notebook that I had stashed in the coffee table last night. My mom has dates when people went missing. Beside them are descriptions of their murders and when the bodies were found.

The murders all started in late May, 2007 and continued until January of this year, 2012. I wonder why they suddenly stopped. Maybe other bodies haven't been found yet. There could be more just lying around somewhere, waiting to be returned to their distraught families.

But there are no references in my mom's notes to any more missing girls after January of 2012. There are dates with names of the missing and a description of how they came to be lost. My mother left empty spaces on the pages that she could fill that in later, when the bodies have been found... if they're ever found.

It's odd how most of these murdered victims were initially taken from British Columbia, then Calgary and finally here in our area. Is the serial killer living here amongst us? Could it be true? Did my mother find out who it is? Is that why she was murdered? Did she get too close to breaking the case wide open?

My fingers start to tingle and stars fill my eyes. I have to remind myself to breathe. My emotions are all over the place. I'm scared, and angry, and sad, but also relieved that I have a lead now. I have something to follow that might give some sort of warped reason why she was murdered.

Realizing the time, I stash the book back in the coffee table then quickly shower, dress and drive to school, arriving just in time for the bell to ring. I get to class and whisper to Billy, who's sitting beside me.

"I read through the other notebook this morning. I think I have something. Can you come over after school?"

"There was another notebook?" Billy looks shocked and maybe a little upset that I read through it without him.

"Yeah, it was at the bottom of the box, under more newspaper clippings." I answer him in a whisper.

Billy rolls his eyes then whispers back. "I made you promise me last night that you wouldn't read through anything else. Did you find out something?"

"I flipped through it this morning. I only promised that I wouldn't read it last night, and I didn't. I had a nightmare and woke up early. I had nothing better to do."

He, curious, asks, "What's in it? What does it say?"

"Just come over after school, okay? I need your help figuring it out. We need to chart out a timeline. This could be why my mother was killed. Maybe she knew too much. Will you help me?"

"Do you think that's such a good idea? What if this killer figures out that you know too much? What do you think he'll do then? Maybe you should just leave it alone, pack it back up and put it away or better yet, burn it."

I look at him like he's crazy. "Yeah right! It's not likely but it's possible that this could be the evidence everyone is looking for. It's probably nothing but who knows, right?"

Billy looks paler than when we first started talking. He nods then draws my attention to the teacher who is now staring at us. I apologize shyly as I open my book.

I truly hate it when people center me out and the whole class is doing just that. You'd think I would have gotten used to it by now but I just can't.

Lunch sucks because I'm forced to eat alone again while too many people glance my way as they sit in their little huddles. When will they ever get past this? It's hard to ignore them. I wish I had the courage to stand up and yell at them to shut the hell up but I don't. I'm not that type of person.

So here I sit, with my text book open, pretending to study. I guess nobody wants to sit with the girl whose mother was murdered. I don't mind, I like my alone time. I just open my book and drift off into my own thoughts or try to read while I eat my nachos and slurp my pop.

CHAPTER 17

Once Billy and I are settled at the kitchen table with our peanut butter sandwiches, we open the notebook that I was talking about in class. We study it silently as we chew and drink our milk to wash down the gooey peanut butter that sticks in our throats.

"Okay, so all we have to do is figure out who moved here just before the girls went missing." I do my best to get my words out clearly but the peanut butter on the roof of my mouth makes that difficult.

Billy added, "And who lived in Calgary. We also have to wonder if maybe your mom did not find out about some other missing girls along the way. I mean, what's to say that the murderer didn't kill girls from somewhere else? Why just these basic areas? There could be lots more out there that nobody knows about from this same killer and they could be from lots of other places around Canada... perhaps even in the United States."

I know where he's going with this. "I wondered the same thing but look at the way the murderer, we'll name him He, took the girls. It's like He has a certain method of operation. All the television shows say they have an MO that they tend to follow. It's what gets them off. It distinguishes them from other serial killers. One of His trademarks could be that He takes them without a struggle. Nobody ever hears a scream or anything."

"So maybe these girls knew their attacker, or at the very least, weren't intimidated by Him. He was able to get close enough to either knock them unconscious or somehow get them to go with him willingly. He can't be scary-looking." Billy says. "Or maybe he's just really strong and can overpower them quickly and easily."

I sarcastically say, "So no scrawny guys and not someone with a hunchback and evil eyes then, huh?" Billy shakes his head and chuckles.

Further into the notebook we see captions of other murders or questionable deaths in these areas but they don't really fit the MO of this killer. Mom must have done her best to decipher which murders belonged to our guy and which didn't because all the deaths from gunshots or stabbings are crossed out. It's only the bodies that were found with evidence of strangulation and sexual assaults that are still listed.

"Okay, so let's try to figure out who moved here around the time the first murder happened in this area." I say as I open a new notebook that has no writing in it. Billy looks at me. I confess, "I can't bring myself to write in her books. If I destroy her writing, her works, the pages she had her

hands on... I will never forgive myself."
Billy just nods.

I draw a timeline and start to fill in who we know of that moved here and when. I start from the spring of 2010, just before the first body was found. With Billy's help, I start writing down names, including his and mine.

Billy told me that they moved here in December of 2009. I know Billy's father could never hurt anyone and the since the disappearances didn't start until May of 2010, I doubt a serial killer could hold off that long between killings. But, what do I know about serial killers? Either way, he's off my radar.

Billy himself is the sweetest person I have ever met. He is so gentle with me that the thought of him hurting me, or any female for that matter, is ridiculous.

The first on our list is the Johnson family. They moved here in April of 2010.

They are a family of three. Andy is the father, Lynne is the mother and Janny is their daughter who would have been four at the time they moved here. They came to this town because he lost his job and heard that they're always looking for loggers in this town. They hail from Southern Ontario. Janny has since become a big sister to a set of twin girls.

In April of 2010, Gary and Bradley Dresden also moved here. They are two brothers who came from Toronto. They were construction workers that also lost their jobs when that company they worked for went belly-up. They came here to do some logging, just like Andy Johnson and so many others before him. I suppose they could be our killers, or maybe just one of them is.

In May of 2010, Lacy Bayler moved here with her two kids, Jeff and Rachel. Her husband was a soldier who had recently died in the war overseas. She moved back here to be closer to her parents. She's originally from this area but had moved to the east coast after she married her husband. I highly doubt that she's a murderer of little girls. Besides, the bodies they found had been raped. So the odds of Lacy being involved are slim at best.

May is when Mom and I came here. Moving into this house was like a dream come true. This was our serenity; our own little chunk of Heaven. Who knew it would turn out to be our little piece of Hell?

In June of 2010, Andrew and Beth Igles moved here for their retirement from London, Ontario. Andrew is so full of arthritis that I doubt he could carry a dead body if someone offered him a million dollars to do it. Besides, they've never lived in Calgary or British Columbia. They spent their lives working and raising six kids, four of which are girls.

"I think we've covered everyone. I can't think of anyone else." I stand up to get

Billy and me a pop from the fridge and notice Jack peering out from around the corner in the hallway. He's baring his teeth quietly and shaking violently.

I laugh and shake my head. "Do you have to go outside, Jack?" His ears perk. I pass Billy on my way to the door and call Jack to come. He growls while he circles the room, staying as far away from Billy as he can, without taking his eyes off of him, until he's safely out the back door. Even so, he doesn't look away for very long. Crazy mutt.

"Your dog hates me." Billy says with a snicker.

"Yeah, well, he always has. But don't take it personally. He doesn't seem to like very many men. When Deputy River Walters was here, he hid from him too."

"Why was he here?" Billy asks.

"He was going through some of my mother's file with me. He's the only authority figure who seems to give a rat's ass about this case. I mean, he's being really nice. He's been keeping me informed when nobody else would. The sheriff doesn't want to give me access to all the details about the investigation even when I beg and plead. I'm just happy to have River around. Even though he isn't giving me all the details, he's giving me most. He's becoming more of a friend than just a cop investigating this case." I'm smiling like a fool. I force myself to stop once I realize that I'm doing it.

With a deeper voice than normal, Billy says, "Well maybe he has a crush on you." He sounds angry or maybe a bit jealous. His lips purse. I know that look. He's upset.

I hand him his pop and laugh when I say, "Sounds like someone is a little jealous." I tease him.

Billy stands up directly in front of me, very closely. While staring deeply into my eyes, he says, "So what if I am?"

He wraps his arms around my waist, pulling me tightly into him. Before I can even resist, his lips are on mine. His mouth is warm and inviting. I pull away and wipe the kiss from my mouth. I walk into the kitchen creating some space between us.

"Why did you do that? We're friends, I mean, we aren't... we can't..." I fight for words but they don't seem to flow very easily.

Billy walks toward me but keeps his distance when I put my hand up to stop him. "Why can't we be more? We already love each other. We're the best of friends. Does the thought of being my girlfriend repulse you that much?"

"I just thought we were friends, only friends. I have never considered you as more than a brother to me. I can't just shift gears and you suddenly become more than that. I'm sorry Billy, but I don't feel the same as you do." I can't look him in the eyes. Now I feel guilty for teasing him about River. I had no idea that he felt this way. I wonder how long he's been contemplating us being lovers.

Billy steps toward me again as if to hug me and I move to the other side of the kitchen shaking my head. "Billy... I can't."

He's angry, hurt and maybe a little embarrassed. Barely holding himself in check, he lowers his voice, and says, "Don't forget to put your heartthrob Deputy Walters on that list. He's a cop, so he'd be a very qualified person on how to get away with murder." I just shake my head.

Jack is clawing and barking frantically at the sliding glass door. He desperately wants in. I quickly go to let him in but stop when I hear the front door slam. Billy has stormed out.

Perhaps I was too cruel. I hope I haven't lost my best friend.

CHAPTER 18

I've been calling Billy and leaving messages all night but haven't gotten a response. He must be really upset not to take my calls. What would I say to him if he picked up that would make it any better? A relationship with him, other than being just friends, is out of the question and giving me the cold shoulder isn't going to sway me in his favor.

Saturday morning I'm at work. Sheriff Johnson and Deputy Walters come in for their breakfast just like any other day. I serve them their coffees and take their orders. On the way back I serve Jill and Beth their breakfasts, hot from the kitchen.

I sit at the table with the sheriff and his deputy. I open the folded up photocopies of a few of my mother's research papers and a copy of my timeline. I stashed them in my pocket earlier this morning in hopes of giving them to Johnson and Walters this morning. On the sheets are the names, dates and descriptions of all the missing and dead that my mother had noted.

They are both fascinated with the in-depth research that my mother had done. I explain what I learned from just reading her notes and ask them to look into the names of the people who moved here around the time the disappearances and murders started.

The sheriff keeps shaking his head. He doesn't believe that this serial killer is the guy we are looking for. He doesn't see a connection other than the fact that my mother was tracking him. He says that there are too many differences in his MO for him to be the same guy. Most serial killers stick to what they know and what they like. Rarely do they veer off in a different direction, for intance, opting to kill a much older woman than his usual choice. But he does agree that it is a coincidence that she was murdered and investigating a killer.

Sheriff Percy asks me to hand over the actual notebooks but I refuse. I know that if I do, I'll most likely never see those books again. I can't risk losing them forever. I promise to get copies of every page for them. Even after the Sheriff threatens to arrest me for impeding an investigation, I hold firm. He mentions that he could get a warrant for them. I tell him to do what he has to.

To my surprise, he backs down, deciding to trust that I'll get the copies for him but only if I allow him access to the actual books even if it's just in my presence. I also promise to give them to him if anything comes of this lead and they are needed in court by the prosecution. They promise to look into it for any possible leads and get back to me if anything arises.

I finish my shift at 4 o'clock after what seems like a neverending day. I was expecting Billy to be here like he usually is after we've had an argument but he's nowhere in sight. He must still be really upset with me.

I call him from my car. It rings three times before he answers. His first words are, "I didn't mean to put you on the spot like that. I'm sorry." He sounds out of breath as if he ran to pick up the phone.

I was expecting 'Hello'. "No, it's not totally your fault. I overreacted. I'm sorry. We should really talk about this. Where are you? I'm just finishing up at work so I can come to you... we can hang out. Are you at home?"

I'm met with a very quick response. "No, I'll meet you at your house later. I'll bring a pizza for dinner... around six o'clock. Sound good?"

"Um, okay, yeah sure." He hangs up before I can say good-bye. I think he's still a little upset, even though he's trying to act all cool about it. At least he still wants to be friends. I just hope he doesn't try to kiss me again.

I put my fingers to my lips, remembering how his felt when they met mine. They were soft, warm. I must admit that I felt loved, very loved. I shake my head to rid the thought. He is my friend, my best friend. He is not my lover.

I head to the grocery store to pick up a few things on my way home. The store is nearly empty aside from a few shoppers, a stock boy that goes to my school and one cashier.

After a polite conversation about the weather with the cashier while she totals my purchases, I carry the bags out to my car and set them in the backseat. I slide in behind the wheel and shut my door.

With the car started and my seatbelt on, I'm just about to put it in reverse when the passenger door flies open and someone hops in. It happens so fast that I can't react quickly enough. I undo my seatbelt and grab the door handle when I suddenly realize who is now sitting in my car with me. It's my father.

"Hello, Pickle!" His voice is terrifyingly familiar to me. My mind instantly starts flashing images of what his temper has caused him to do. Fear.

He continues talking loudly but in a happy manner. "You are a hard girl to track down. I have been looking everywhere for you. I actually had to hire someone to help me hunt you down. Can you believe that?"

He hunted me down? My body feels so cold, like ice is running through my veins instead of hot blood. Is he going to kill me like a hunter would his prey? I stare at him, to afraid to run.

"What's the matter with you? Cat got your tongue?" He laughs. "Well now say something. I've traveled a long way to get here. Shouldn't you give your dear old daddy a hug?"

I stutter out, "Nnn... No! What... What are you doing here? How did you find me? How did you get out of jail?" I'm yelling at him, still too scared to run.

He lowers his voice making him sound scarier. "Well now, calm down! Don't be yelling at your father. You will respect me, young lady." His face is serious and very intimidating. I remember that look from back when I was younger and he was getting ready to hit my mom.

"I'm sorry, you scared me." I say trying to calm the situation down before he completely loses his temper. I remember how easily that used to happen. It was like flipping on a light switch, only it was his temper; on then off, mean then sweet.

"I didn't mean to scare you. I've been waiting for a chance to get you alone and well, this was a prime opportunity." He looks around nervously.

"You should go. The cops are looking for you. You skipped out on your parole visits. Did you know that there's a warrant out for your arrest?" I say with a shaky voice.

"I figured as much. But, I'm like a fox and they can't catch me." He laughs. He puts a cigarette in his mouth but before he can light it, I beg him not to smoke in my car. He takes it out of his mouth and slides it up over his ear letting his greasy hair cover it.

"What do you want?" I ask him.

He breathes out a long sigh before speaking. "Whatever happened to 'Hi Daddy, I missed you'? Didn't you miss me at all?"

"To be completely honest, no I did not. It's been quiet without you around and

I've liked that very much. So you should just leave. I don't want you in my life again." I say without looking at him. I wait nervously for that hard back-hand that he used to give my mother when she said things like that to him. To my surprise, it doesn't come.

"I'm not staying long. Don't you worry, even if I wanted to the cops will catch me if I'm not constantly on the move. I just had to see you, Pickle. I missed you every day. I did what I could to be a good little boy in prison so that I could get out and come see you; my sweet, adorable little girl. I suppose you're not so little anymore though, huh? Look at you; you're a beautiful young woman now."

He brushes the hair back from my face but I slap his hand away and glare at him. "Just go. Please just get out of my car and leave me alone." Tears start to run from the corners of my eyes. "Don't ever come back."

He chooses to ignore my pleas. "How's your Momma doing? Why don't you put this car into gear and take me to see her? I miss seeing her sweet face so very much too. I should probably bring her some flowers or something and I should definitely apologize for being such a bastard to her before I got locked up. I do understand why she testified against me. I do not like it, but I can see why she did it. I forgive her."

I stare at him, trying to decide if he said those things to make me angry, try to make a cover for himself if in fact he killed her, or maybe he truly doesn't know that she's dead. He tilts his head and looks at me blank faced. "What? You look like you've seen a ghost."

"She's dead, Dad. Someone murdered her. Just how long have you been in town? Did you do it? Did you lose your temper again, only this time you didn't stop before you killed her? Did you exact your revenge for her damning testimony that helped put you away?" I'm so angry right now I could kill him myself.

The blood drains from his face. He looks like he's going to throw up. He whispers as though he has no breath left in his body. "She's dead? I didn't know. I'm sorry Pickle. I should have been here to protect her." He looks out the window and mumbles something to himself. When he turns back to look at me, he eyes are red and glossy. "Who did it? Who killed her? When did this happen?"

"So you didn't know? How long have you been in town?" I ask again.

Dad keeps shaking his head back and forth until he slaps the dashboard so hard that I jump and screech.

"Dammit! No, Pickle, I just got to town yesterday. I had no idea, I swear!" he proclaims with his hand in the air as if he's making a vow. "For God's sake, tell me, when did this happen?"

"About a month ago. I'm fine by the way. Believe me when I tell you that I did not need you... I'll never need you. You have to go and no matter what, don't ever come back." My voice is clear and sure: he has to know that I mean every word.

Dad looks as if I've shattered his world. "I'm sorry, Pickle. I've made a lot of mistakes in my life but you were never one of them. You are the best thing that I ever did and ever will do. The worst thing I ever did was start drinking all those years ago. If I had never have drank a single sip, I'm sure my life would have taken a better path. But I can't change the past. I can only repent for it."

I stare out the windshield of the car, avoiding his eyes. I don't believe he's a changed man. How can someone with that much anger ever learn to hold it back,? I've seen his rage and I doubt that it can ever be contained. Who's he trying to convince: me or himself?

"I'll go now. I hope that someday you can forgive me for the wrongs I've done. I'm not drinking anymore; haven't touched booze since that day I killed that guy. Even after I got out of prison I didn't drink anything, not one damn drop."

"You need to go," is all I can say.

Dad pauses briefly and looks out the passenger window. "Yeah I know. I love you, Katie. I always will. Nothing will ever change that. Can you point me in the direction of the police station? Now that I've completed my objective to see you, I think I'm ready to go back and finish my sentence. I just needed to know that you were okay."

"You purposely skipped your parole appointments so you could track me down?" I say while debating whether to drive him to the sheriff's office personally but realizing that I don't want him in my car that long. I point down the street. "Down there, first street on the left."

"Thanks and yeah, I skipped so I could find you. I couldn't wait through two years of probation and having to stick around that area. I had to find you. You and your mom are all I thought about when I was locked up. Even though you doubt it, I love you and your mom more than anything in this world. Maybe one day you'll see that and let me be a part of your life again." He puts his hand on my shoulder and I shrug it off. "I love you, Pickle. Take care of yourself. It's obvious that you don't want me in your life right now. I'll leave it up to you to reconnect with me someday. If you change your mind and want to see me, I'm sure you will be able to track me down."

He climbs out of my car, shuts the door and starts walking down the street in the direction I pointed out to him. I doubt that he's really turning himself in. I don't care if he does or not, as long as he's far away from me.

I realize my hands are shaking as I quickly lock the doors. I put the car in drive and hurry home.

CHAPTER 19

When I get there, Deputy Walters is waiting in his car, drinking a hot coffee. He steps out when I pull in the driveway.

"Hello, Katie. I knew you'd be home soon because your shift ends at 4:00 on Saturdays." I'm surprised he knows that. "I looked into your mother's notes and questioned a few people on the list. Everyone seems to check out but there are some things I'd like to ask you... if you're not busy, of course. Are you all right?"

I must be pale as a ghost. "Um, my father was just in my car at the grocery store. He came out of nowhere. He opened the passenger door and climbed. Scared the crap out of me." My hands are still a little shaky.

The Deputy quickly hops in his car and radios the Sheriff. While waiting for him to respond, he asks me, "It's going to be okay, Katie." I nod my head. "Do you know where he went when he got out?"

"I sent him in the direction of the Sheriff's office. He said he was turning himself in but I truly doubt he was actually going to do it." I say.

Sheriff Percy Johnson informs the deputy that my father just walked into their office and turned himself over to their custody. He and an RCMP officer are questioning him right now.

I look at River and quietly say, "I don't think he killed my mom. I know my dad and the way he reacted to the news of her death, tells me that he had no idea. He didn't kill her. I'm sure of it."

River signs off the CB radio and shuts the car door. "Is it all right if I come in with you? I'd like to talk to you about the information you gave to us earlier. If you think now is a good time. I mean, you look pretty shaken up. I'm sure having someone sit with you for a little while couldn't hurt." He pauses. "I could always come back later."

"Um, no, now is fine. I don't have any plans until dinner time. Come on in." I say as I unlock the front door. Jack jumps up on me, happy that I'm home. Until he sees that Deputy Walters is right behind me. He scurries with his tail between his legs to the glass doors at the back of the house. I drop my purse and hang up my coat before letting Jack outside.

I gesture for River to sit at the table. "I'm having a pop. Would you like one?"

He holds up his coffee. "No, thank you. I'm set."

He makes his way over to the kitchen table and hangs his coat on the back of the chair before sitting. I never noticed before that River is really cute. He isn't wearing his baggy uniform today. His t-shirt is snug-fitting against his firm chest and flat stomach. His jeans fit tightly to his strong thighs. I never considered River to be an actual guy. I've never thought of him in any way other than as a cop. Right now he looks like just a regular, hot twenty-three year old guy, not an authority figure.

"Are you okay?" River wakes me from my train of thought, probably because I was ogling his body.

"Ah, yeah, sorry. What were you saying?" I feel my cheeks flush. He caught me staring. I'm so embarrassed.

He tries to hide a smile by turning his head but it's obvious by his reaction that he saw me looking at him while thinking sexy thoughts. "I wanted to let you know what I've been up to all afternoon."

"You aren't wearing your uniform. Is it at the cleaners?" I joke nervously.

He smiles, nervously, "No, ah, today is actually my day off."

"And you're working on my mother's case? Dedicated aren't you?" I have a whole new appreciation for River.

He smiles, nods then opens the folder he carried into the house. "Nobody really strikes a nerve with me. We can assume the murderer is a male because all of his victims had evidence of sexual activity; whether rape or consensual, we may never know. There's never any DNA left on or in any cavities of the victims. We know that He washes them before he dumps them."

"We should give Him a title, kind of like the Green River Killer's. It'll be easier for us than having to say He or Him all the time."

"How about we just call him 'Him' or 'He' for now? Nicknaming serial killers gives them validation and I don't think they deserve to be acknowledged with that kind of attention. I believe it just glorifies them. Cops never name them, the media does." River says.

I nod, feeling foolish. "That makes sense." I change the subject. "So you said that you talked to people on the list."

"I did talk to some. I went to see Andy Johnson at his work site but he couldn't spend much time chatting because he was busy with something time-sensitive. I doubt he has anything to do with these girls' deaths. Call it a gut feeling." River flips the page to the next person on the list.

"I was wondering about Gary and Bradley Dresden because they're originally from British Columbia. Did you get a chance to interview them?" I ask.

"Just Gary. Bradley is out of town at a doctor's appointment today. He had to see a specialist for his left hand. I'm not sure if you heard about happened. His hand was crushed last week in a terrible accident. His brother told me that a log swung back at Bradley, crushing his hand between it and another tree. He broke eight bones. Gary says that it's really bad and that the doctors don't think he'll be able to work as a logger anymore." River shakes his head, sadly. "I feel awful for the guy. I'd spoken to him at the cafe some time ago. He seems like a pleasant, very hard working guy."

"That's horrible. I heard someone say something about it but I don't pay much attention to gossip at work anymore. I've learned to ignore people since my mother's death and the gossip is mostly about me anyway." I squeeze my lips together and shake my head. "I try not to let it bother me but it still hurts when people say things about me or my mom, especially if most of it isn't even true." I think about Anna's cruel ways.

"Sorry about that. People can be so mean." River seems genuine. I just nod. "Okay, so in my opinion, I don't think Gary would hurt a fly. He's so focussed on working and making money that I doubt he'd take the time it would require to kidnap, hold captive, rape, beat and murder

247

young girls. This killer likes to keep them alive for about a week for whatever sick fantasy he feels a need to play out."

I get up and let Jack back in the house. He quickly slinks around the front room until he's hiding in his bed, growling softly, refusing to take his sights away from River.

River chuckles as he watches Jack. "I think he's readying himself to leap to your rescue if I were to suddenly attack you."

"Yeah well, he's been especially nervous around men ever since..." For some reason I can't finish the sentence. I feel so bad for Jack.

"Understandable. Some say that dogs are a good judge of character." His deep green eyes meet mine and my stomach flips in a nervous way. He looks away quickly. "I'll have a chat with Bradley Dresden when he returns but I doubt he's involved either. Lacy is not even a candidate for this because she's a female and also way too tiny to carry the weight of a dead child for any great distance. Andrew and Beth Igles are also off the table because he couldn't lift a baby let alone a teenager. His arthritis won't allow it. Beth doesn't weigh more than a hundred pounds herself so carrying a body to clean up after her husband is out of the question."

I shrug, feeling defeated. "Well that only leaves Billy's family and me. I know I didn't kill her. Billy's family would never, ever hurt my mom. I know them. His dad is a psychiatrist and his mom... well she's female so that rules her out. Billy would have been only twelve or thirteen years old when the murders started in British Columbia and I doubt anyone that young would be able to pull off something like that without getting caught. Billy is really smart but I don't think he's that smart. But then again, I have seen pictures of him when he was younger and he was always a big kid for his age. Even though he would have had the strength to pull it off... it's Billy, he could never do that to anyone."

"Maybe so but they did live in BC when the murders started. And, they did live here when the local murders began happening. If you are right and Billy has always been big for his age, carrying the weight of one of these girls would have been difficult for him but not impossible. All of these victims had a small stature." River says.

"Okay but they never lived in Calgary. Billy would have told me. He's my best friend. He tells me everything." There's no way I'm going to let River start a manhunt for Billy or his father. The thought of either one of them murdering a girl sounds utterly ridiculous. "When did you move here?" I'm shifting the conversation his way.

River looks up from the paperwork and our eyes meet. "January of 2010. I came from Toronto."

"I'm not accusing you. I'm just saying that your name should also be on the list because you did move here within the timeframe of the first murder, just like Billy's family and the others did." I gesture for him to write in his name. He writes his name in but shakes his head with a smirk while he does it.

"Okay, I've written myself down as a suspect. Are you happy?" He looks up at me and grins.

He really is a great-looking guy. I look away quickly. "Yes. I suppose I am."

"I've never lived in Calgary." River adds.

"How do I know that? Do you have proof?" I say jokingly.

"Do you need proof?" He jokes back.

"I might." I fold my arms across my chest and raise one eyebrow.

River chuckles while closing the folder. "I'll get out of your way. I just thought you should know how things are coming along." River stands beside me at the front door. I open it but he doesn't step out right away. "Be careful who you talk to about this. We should keep this between us and Sheriff Johnson. At least until I have thoroughly investigated everyone... including myself." He smiles.

"I'll ask Billy about Calgary in a roundabout way so he doesn't think I'm onto him. But I already know the answer. They've never lived there. It would have come out at some point during the last few years." I say with conviction.

"Why don't you leave that to me? It is my job." He says in a very serious manner.

"Yeah but he's my friend."

River awkwardly puts his arm around my shoulders and gives me a quick but cozy hug. As he leaves he trips over the last step and nearly falls. Without looking back, he waves his hand to assure me that he's all right then gets into his car and drives away, shaking his head, leaving me wondering what that was all about.

CHAPTER 20

Billy shows up just after six o'clock with a large pizza. We sit on the sofa and eat while we watch television. Not much is said until we've finished our first slice.

"You said that you lived in British Columbia but I was wondering if you've ever lived anywhere else?" I try to act as though I'm not interrogating him.

Billy looks at me, smiles and says, "Not for any length of time. Why do you ask?"

"No particular reason. I was just curious. I've been thinking about how a lot of the people who live in this town originate from somewhere else." I look back down at my pizza for a moment then add, "So like where have you lived, even if it was only for a week?"

"Why do you want to know so badly? Where's this really coming from?" He asks as he looks directly at me, causing me to feel a quiver of nervousness. The last thing I want to do is piss him off again. I should be apologizing for reacting so badly to his kissing me, not drilling him about something as dumb as River's assumption that the murderer could be a member of Billy's family.

"I'm just trying to make conversation. I haven't lived anywhere interesting. You know all about me, so I thought it'd be nice to know more about you, for once." I say, trying to seem as casual as I can.

He takes a sip of his pop. "Hmm, you're right. I don't think we have talked much about me. I suppose there's no reason not to tell you now that you've told me all about your dad. Besides, it's not like I've been purposely concealing anything about where my family has been. It just never really came up in conversation before. I've lived in every province from BC to Ontario.

My parents like to move around a lot. They say it keep things fresh."

"You have? Really? Which place was your favorite?" I ask.

"Well that's a silly question. Here, of course. I have you here." He smiles ear to ear.

I roll my eyes and laugh but wonder if this is going to be the start of another argument about us dating.

"Wait a minute. Does this have to anything to do with those notebooks you're reading through?" he asks.

I take a long sip of my pop to stall. No matter how hard I try to think of some lie to tell him, I can't think of anything but the truth. "I was figuring out the timeline for those girl's murders and got curious about some things. I looked into the dates of when people moved to this town to see who matches up. This is going to sound really crazy. Just hear me out for a minute, okay? From what you've told me about your family's moving history, it fits in the timeframe and I just want to rule your dad out as one of the potential suspects."

"Are you serious?" Billy's face looks ashen. His expression is one of shock.

I feel a pang of guilt in the pit of my stomach. How awful of me to doubt my best friend's father.

I stand up and walk to the kitchen. "It's just that... I mean, you were a young teenager when the murders started in British Columbia so that makes you an unlikely suspect. But your dad... well, he does fit the profile, I suppose. I just mean that he is physically capable. By no means do I think he did it. I just want to be able to scratch your family off the list, that's all."

Billy gets up and follows me. "You think... you think my dad is capable of murdering little girls?" He tries to laugh it off but his smile fades quickly. I can tell he's a really hurt by my accusation.

"No, not really. I mean, because I know your dad and love him more than my own father, he is the least likely suspect on that list. But, I need you to tell me if you ever lived in Calgary because if you haven't then there's no reason to continue this conversation." I'm getting frustrated now. Why won't he just tell me if his dad ever lived in Calgary?

Maybe River was right. Bringing this up to Billy started off badly and is getting worse. I should have just kept my mouth shut to begin with. I've only managed to hurt Billy's feelings and possibly ruin our friendship forever. I wish I could rewind time.

"So you do think that it could be me." he says sharply. "You must if you are so sure that my father couldn't be the bad guy. That only leaves me, right?"

I stand before my friend, staring into his eyes, just looking for some sign, a facial twitch, anything to give him away but there's nothing. How could I have ever thought for one second that he could harm anyone? I shake my head. What was I thinking? It's Billy after all. He's the kindest person I know.

I exhale my words heavily. "No, I don't. I was wrong to bring this up. You wouldn't hurt a fly neither would your father."

Billy smiles at me. "Oh don't be fooled little girl, I've hurt many flies in my years." He winks at me as though to forgive me for the ridiculous accusations.

Then I get serious and ask him. "Why did you kiss me like that?"

"It just felt right at the time." He replies matter-of-factly.

"I don't understand. We've been friends, best friends -- just best friends, for two years. Why ruin a good thing by turning it into something that it's not meant to be? I mean, why now?" I ask.

He looks over at me with an expression that I don't understand. It's not anger or disappointment, or even embarrassment. He seems almost numb. "I want to be more than just your best friend. I need to be." He runs his fingers through his hair. He does that when he's nervous or worried. "You are very important to me in so many more ways than you can ever know. Please don't be angry with me. I don't do well when I can't be around you. You keep me sane when I'm with you. I completely fall apart when we fight."

I roll my eyes, "I keep you sane? Really? I'm not the shrink in your family, your dad is and I don't think you've ever been insane, with me or not." I laugh. Billy goes to say something but I cut him off.

"Look, we can't be together in that way. I love you like a brother. Siblings don't date each other. Can we just get past this and go back to the way we were before the kiss?" I walk back into the living room.

Billy stands quietly for a moment. "Do you think we can ever be together? Like, maybe in the future sometime?"

I pick up the pizza box up from the living room table and take it into the kitchen. While shoving the box in the fridge, I answer him. "I don't know. But, as I see things right now, I'd have to say no. I love you Billy, just not the way you want me to."

CHAPTER 21

I wake in the dark with dizzying head pain. It hurts differently from a migraine. Words echo at first as if someone is talking through a really bad phone. Slowly the words clear up, sharpening to the point where I can understand them. I open my heavy eyelids and see a blurry vision of a girl leaning over me.

Her voice is soft and kind. "Are you all right? You've been out cold since he brought you here. What's your name?"

Confusion. I can't remember anything that happened. I have no idea where I am and I can't get the room to stop spinning long enough to figure it out. Wait, this isn't a room, at least not one that I've ever been in. It smells musty like the ground after a light rain but it's arid, like a desert. There isn't much heat, only a chill in the air that sends shivers up my spine.

My mouth is dry, so dry that when I attempt to swallow, my tongue sticks in my throat. I gag and choke. I blink several times trying to focus on the face leaning over me. My eyes wander despite my efforts to hold them still. My ears still hum with every word she speaks as if I'm lying with my head under the water in a bathtub.

"Here, drink this." The kind girl holds a cup to my lips and I gulp a mouthful, then another. The cool water washes my throat, soothing my vocal cords.

"What... happened?" I try to sit up but when the nauseating dizziness hits, I'm forced back down on the cot. "Where am I? How'd I get here?" I make another failed attempt at sitting up. It causes my head to swirl and the water I gulped to rise in my throat.

"Here's a bucket," the unfamiliar girl says. I vomit into the bucket with enough force to empty all the undigested pizza from my stomach. My throat is not only drier than it was a few minutes ago but it's also sore.

"Lie back and relax. Take your time. I was the same way when I first got here. It only lasts for a few hours. I think he hit your head to knock you out because you have the same lovely bump that I do. My mom would say that you have a concussion. She's a nurse." She pauses while she places the bucket on the floor. "So, what's your name?"

The dizziness is subsiding enough where I can clearly make out her face. She's younger than I, about fifteen years old. Her eyes are puffy, clear evidence that she's been crying. Her lip is cut and she has a large purple bruise on her left cheek and neck.

"Um, I'm Katie. Who are you?"

"My name is Anita. Anita Tristan."

"How long have you been here? Wait, where is here?" I ask, slowly looking around so as not to bring back the spins.

"I think I got here yesterday, maybe it was two days ago. I really don't know." The tears that flow slowly down her face highlight purple bruise on her cheek. "My parents must be out of their minds with worry."

I put my hand on her arm to try and comfort her. She looks like she's scared to death. She places her hand over mine and pats it as if she's trying to comfort me even though she's the one crying.

I groan loudly as I slowly sit up. The room spins around me even after I plant my feet firmly on the ground. I hold the edges of the cot tightly with both hands, taking in long breaths with my eyes focused on the floor until the room slows.

"Are you okay now? Are you going to throw up again?" she asks me.

265

I lift my head slowly so I can take in my surroundings, hoping to find a way out. "Nah, I'm all right."

My jeans have blood on them. I start to examine my arms and legs for cuts and I'm surprised to find no injuries aside from the obvious one on the back of my head. "Whose blood is this?"

"I don't know. You both had blood on you when he brought you here. He didn't look to be too badly injured but he had a scarf wrapped around his hand." She stares off, lost in thought. "That's all I know. I tried not to stare at him."

"I can't remember how I got here. Everything is so fuzzy." I say to her as I rub the lump on my head.

"I had the same confusion as you. When I first woke up, I couldn't remember anything after having breakfast with my mother. It took some time before I could remember everything that happened before I blacked out." she explains. I get a sense of hopelessness in her words, not so much by the words themselves but the tone in which she speaks them. She's started to give up hope on ever seeing her mom again.

The walls are rock. There are two candles lit just outside the wall of bars that keeps us captive in this room. It's like a primeval prison. It's damp, cold and light from the candles barely touches the darkness.

"There's no way out, is there?" I ask her.

"If there was, I wouldn't be here." Anita says, tears beginning once again. A long moment of silence fills the room before she cries out, "He raped me. I fought him but he hit me. I was stunned and couldn't fight back after that. He... he hurt me so..." Her voice quivers and fades until only her lips move.

I pull her into my chest and let her weep. I don't want to imagine what this poor girl has gone through. A ghastly thought grips me... what if I'm next? Tears start to pool in my eyes but I blink them away. I tell myself that I am way too angry to cry. With everything Anita has gone through, she was still there to help me when I was coming to. I have to be strong for her. I cannot let him hurt this girl again.

"Who is he?" I ask her.

"I have no idea." She sobs.

"We have to fight him when he comes back in here. Will you help me fight him? It may be our only chance to get away. We can't let him hurt you again." I slowly stand and move the bucket as far away from us as possible then walk the perimeter, clutching the wall to stop from falling down when the room breaks into random spins.

"Wait a minute, I remember something. Last night I was talking to Billy.

Something happened and I fell into the fridge. I think I hit my head. I must have tripped. In an instant, my head felt like it was going to erupt into the worse migraine ever. I remember seeing white stars clouding my vision until everything dissolved into a blinding light. I obviously became unconscious." I'm still confused as to what happened between then and now that landed me here.

"What else do you remember?" she asks.

"Nothing. I mean, that's all I remember until I woke up here with you standing over me. How did I get here? Not Billy... no, it can't be. Oh my God!"

"Who's Billy?" Anita asks anxiously.

"Tell me what he looks like... the guy, what does he look like?" I'm hoping beyond all hope that Billy isn't our captor. Maybe he was trying to stop me from finding out his family's secret. Could it be true that his dad is the monster that my mom got too close to discovering?

"He's not very tall, for a guy, I mean, but he's thick, strong. He's average, I guess. Blonde hair. Creepy brown eyes that I was forced to look into when he was... inside me. I don't know his name. He's just really, really strong." Anita pulls her legs into her chest and wraps her arms around them, resting her head on her knees.

River was right. He told me to be careful who I trusted. Ajax Richardson could see the truth even if he was looking through the bloodshot eyes of a drunkard. How stupid and blinded am I?

Billy must be protecting his father's secret because Billy can't possibly be the killer. There's no way. I love him, he's my best friend and I would know. He could never hurt anyone. I just don't understand why he's chosen his father's evilness over the bonded friendship that we have. Will he let his father do away with me?

I wonder if anyone will figure out that I'm missing before it's too late. Will River put two and two together? Will he find us before Billy's father comes to strangle away our lives? Will Billy be able to talk his father down? After I denied him any hope of a mutual love, will he even want to?

I run to the bucket and vomit again but this time it's not from the concussion. I can't believe that I trusted him. How could he have done the horrible things that he's done and yet Billy still wants to protect him? How did I not know about it?

Worse yet, how could he kill my mother? Why her? And in such a gruesome way! She doesn't fit the profile. How did he find out that she was even looking at his father as the perpetrator? I have so many questions.

"I know the name of the guy who brought me here. He was my best friend. His name is Billy." I take a seat on the cot beside Anita and put my arm gently around her shoulders, pulling her into me. She wraps her arms around me, holding on tightly.

She sobs, "I hate him!"

"As you should." I rub her back.

CHAPTER 22

I ask her, "Can you tell me when you were taken and from where? Tell me everything you remember."

Anita quietly explains. "It seems like I've been here forever. It was Friday when he took me. My mom sent me to the corner store, not far from my house just before dinner. I walked because it's only a few blocks away. I came out of the store after I bought some milk for her and a chocolate bar for me. I started walking home and got about two blocks away when a car drove past me then stalled. The guy got out and lifted the hood to look at the engine. He looked upset. He made me nervous. You know what I mean, that little twitch in your stomach that tells you something's wrong? Well, I should have listened to it but I had to walk past him to get home. It was still daylight so I felt safe enough. Once I got past him, I was relieved but then I heard a loud thud that sounded like it came from within my head. I'm pretty sure that he hit me with something. I must have blacked out. The next thing I know, I'm waking up here and he's taking my pants off. I started hitting and kicking him but I got really dizzy and threw up. Some got on him and he went mad. He put his hand around my throat and squeezed so hard that I couldn't breathe let alone yell for help. I got really weak and I couldn't fight back anymore. He eased off his grip and told me he didn't want to kill me. He said that if I would just be still, he would not kill me. He got between my legs and..."

I pull her tighter to me and rock her slowly. What else can I do? "It's going to be okay. You don't have to tell me any more."

"I have to tell someone. He umm, started to enter me. That's when I fought really hard even though he ordered me not to. I couldn't help it. It hurt so much. I screamed really loud and he slapped my face so hard that I saw stars. He made me look into his eyes the whole time." She pauses for a minute. "When he was finished, he slapped my face again and called me a whore. I was relieved when he left me alone. I prayed for him to never come back. I would rather die of starvation than go through that again."

I seethe with anger. "I am so sorry. How old is this son of a bitch that did that to you?"

"A little older... than us." Her answer makes me leap off the cot and across the room. I don't want to believe her. I mean, obviously I can't doubt her but the realization of her accusation is terrifying.

"This is just too much. I mean, I've been Billy's best friend for two years. He's never gotten really angry about anything. He's always been so gentle. I just don't understand."

"How could you not know he was so evil? He's the one who brought you down here, so, why are you here if he's supposed to be your best friend? Did you piss him off or something?" Anita asks.

"Yeah, I did. My mother was a writer. She was murdered not long ago. I found some notes that she had written and hidden. Apparently she had been tracking a serial killer. She followed the trail of bodies and it led here, to this town. Thinking Billy to be the sweet and caring teenager that he portrayed himself to be, she must have come to the same wrong conclusion that I did, that Billy's father was the killer. Knowing her, she confronted Billy about it, trying to soften the blow before she went to the cops. He must have killed her to her keep her quiet."

Horror grips me, I grasp my chest. If my heart could actually explode in my chest, I don't think it would hurt more than this. Billy... my confidant, the closest thing I ever had to a brother -- is a murderer? Can it be true?

Fear quickly overtakes pain. My muscles stiffen and my body shakes. I want to run but there isn't anywhere to go. I'm frozen in horror. I know what he does to his victims. I've seen his work first hand. Am I next? Is Anita? I can't tell her what's in store for us, it would be too cruel.

"Bodies? Oh my God! He really is going to kill us." She starts shaking so hard that her words come out in a stutter. "How did he kill the other people? I mean, how are we going to die? Please, please tell me that it'll be fast."

Even if I wanted to answer, the ability to form words has escaped me. This can't be happening. I start screaming as loudly as I can, to either wake myself up from this nightmare, or if this truly is real, for someone to hear my pleas and come to save us. Over and over again, I yell until my voice is hoarse. Billy is smart enough not to bring us to a place where people could hear us scream. My legs give way and I slide down the bars to the floor in a spent heap, sobbing quietly.

Soft footsteps approach me. "I'm sorry. I know he was your best friend and I don't want you to think that I'm blaming you for this because this is not your fault. I'm really sorry about your mom. Maybe it was someone else who killed her. This could just be some weird coincidence."

"No, it was him... different MO, same result. How could I be so stupid? How could I not see?" I wipe away the tears. No more self-pity. We have to get angry, now, if we are going to survive this.

"He left a sandwich and some water. I've been afraid to eat or drink, in case he drugged it. You can have some if you want to risk it." Despite everything she's been through, she's trying to help me deal with my emotional pain. What a strong girl.

If things get bad enough, eating a drugged sandwich might be our best option.

I would only hope that there would be enough drugs in it to kill us both. It might be a more humane way to go.

CHAPTER 23

I believe an entire day has passed. It feels like an eternity. There is no way to judge time in this prison. One candle has burnt out and the other can't have more than an hour left on it.

We've passed the time by talking about our families and getting to know one another. No matter how long we talk, time seems to stand still. We have become each other's rock. For now, we are best friends.

How long will we wait here and what exactly are we waiting for? Will he return, forcing us to give into his cruel fantasies or will we be brave enough to fight back? Or are we just simply waiting for something that may never come? Will we die waiting?

Suddenly a noise from outside startles us. My ears strain to hear anything over the pounding of my heart. Footsteps draw closer. Terrified, Anita cowers in the corner beside the cot, shaking and crying.

Fight or flight. What would my mother do? She would fight with everything she has. I silently beg her to give me strength. I stand right up to the bars, knees shaking from fear, or maybe it's anger. He approaches, stopping just out of reach, with an unfamiliar expression on his face.

His eyes are cold and hollow as if his soul is dead. He stands, his expression that of a stranger - cold, without fear or compassion. This person looks like Billy, but this is not the best friend I've known. No, this an evil spirit, empty of humanity. How can I play on his sympathies if he has none?

Without a word, he takes two candles out of a paper bag, lights them then switches them with the two burnt-out wax nubs. I'm a little relieved to know that we won't be sitting here in pitch blackness.

I ask him, as calmly as I can, "Why are you doing this? What's it about?"

He looks at me with his soulless eyes. "You were getting too close. Why did you have to find that box filled with your mother's research? I looked everywhere for her notes. She called me to say that she was investigating a serial killer and she thought it was my father. She called me to talk about it. I don't think she wanted me to be surprised if the cops came to haul my dad in for questioning and possibly arrest him. She was just about to hand over her findings to the police. She said that she loved me and didn't want me hurt by all this. I asked her if I could come over so we could discuss it further. She thought it was a good idea. Well, she was dead wrong. Pardon the pun." He ends in a throaty chuckle.

"Did you kill her? Did you slit her throat?" I ask with so much rage in my voice that I don't recognize the sound.

"I had to. I couldn't let her lead the cops to us. Please try to see it from my point of view." He speaks as though he thinks I will understand and will be okay with it. "If I didn't stop her from going to the cops, she would have ruined everything. Of course my dad would have taken the blame to keep his only son out of prison. It would have been awful for my mother. And, of course, you would hold it against me and our friendship would immediately end. We would have been separated. I couldn't have that. I need you and you need me, even though you don't realize it yet. We have to stay together. We belong to one another. Deep down, you do know that, don't you?"

"Does your father know about your... tendencies?" I ask with a shaking voice.

He laughs so casually. "Yeah he does. He's been trying me on different medications that might control my urges but..." he shrugs, "only being with you stops them. Don't you get it? That's why I said we had to be together. I don't need to hurt people when I'm with you. You make me happy. You fill me up, so to speak. So you see you can't leave me, ever. I need you."

"You say that I'm enough for you... you lie. I know that only two bodies have been found but four girls from our surrounding area have gone missing in the time that we've been friends. If I'm enough, like you say, then why take those four girls?" I ask, trying to prove him wrong.

He shakes his head. "No, no. Think back to those dates. You don't remember, do you? How can you remember? I mean, sometimes you can be so self-absorbed. In June, two years ago, you had just moved here and we weren't quite friends yet. I liked you, a lot, and you didn't even notice me, so I had some frustrations to work out. Obviously, I couldn't play with you so I found a look-alike. She was entertaining. Feisty! She satisfied the urge."

I want to vomit. "What made you decide that you couldn't 'play' with me?"

He tilts his head and looks at me like I'm stupid. "Think about it, Katie. If I took you and played with you, I would have to make sure you didn't tell anyone. That would mean that I would have to kill you. If I had killed you, I wouldn't have you in my life anymore. What fun is that? I just knew that eventually I would win you over and you would be mine... forever. And look, here you are -- mine, forever. But this is not how I pictured our future."

He pauses for a moment and rubs his forehead as though he's stressed. He paces back and forth. His tone shifts to angry and loud, making me jump back from the bars nervously. I hear Anita cry out in fear. "Why did you have to read through that damn book? I told you not to! I knew your mother had notes about the murders that would lead to my family. I couldn't find them and I did look almost everywhere that night. I should have looked in the attic but I never thought that she'd go to that much trouble to hide it. Damn it, Katie! You never listen to me!"

Swallowing my fear, I step up to the bars again. "What about the other three girls?"

"We had a big fight about you wanting to date that jock. You must remember, the one you thought was cute. He was a jerk and I told you he was but you didn't listen. Do you remember? You were so angry at me for being right that you didn't talk to me for over a week. That was in November. I took a girl to entertain me in your absence. We played for nearly 2 weeks, but like the others, she eventually succumbed to her injuries. She wasn't as fun as her predecessor but she was a good listener. I told her all about you."

"And the other two?" I'm so disgusted. If I could get my hands on him right now I might scratch his eyes out.

I just can't believe that this evil monster standing before me, who looks like my best friend, isn't. Who is this bastard? What happened to him that made him so awful? Why didn't I see it?

So many questions and doubts are running through my mind. I try to think back to the incidents that he's talking about and he's right, I did ignore him because I was upset with him. It was easy to do because he was never around after we would argue. He just stayed away. Back then I just thought that he was at home licking his wounds. How could I be so naive?

He shakes his head. "Despite what you think, I'm not unreasonable. I only took one other girl and that was last January. You took that trip to Toronto with your mom for her books. My father was trying out a new drug on me and well, it failed miserably. I needed you but you weren't here. I took someone else instead. What choice did I have? I would have gone crazy otherwise. She only lasted two days. She was weak. She wasn't a good substitute for you at all. What a huge waste of my energy. I was so disappointed. I don't know who took the other missing girl but it wasn't me."

"So what are you going to do with us? Are you going to kill us too?" I stare him right in the eyes with my chin held high even though every cell in my body is afraid. I want him to open the bars so I can rip his face off. I want to beat him to a bloody pulp but fear holds me trembling where I stand.

"Aren't you hearing me? I don't want to kill you, Katie. I love you. It's just a matter of time before you love me too, you'll see. As for her," he lifts his face and looks toward Anita. "I haven't decided yet. For our safety, I can't let her go because she's seen my face. She's seen you as well. I can't let her tell on us. I don't want you to get into trouble."

I'm confused. Why does he think I'm part of whatever he's doing here with Anita? In his twisted way of seeing the world, he must think I'm his cohort. He really is sick.

Angrily, I say, "How can I get into trouble? You kidnapped me!" His confused expression tells me that he does think we are partners in crime. I have to try to act the way he believes I should. He's obviously delusional. "We could keep her. I don't mind. I mean, it can't hurt to think of her as our love child. Or better yet, I've always wanted a little sister. At the very least, she'll keep me company when you're not around."

"Our love child? Seriously? What do you think I am, stupid? We've never even made love. It's made up, so of course you can't believe it. That's ridiculous. I tell you what, you give a little and I'll give a little too. I'll make you a deal; you have to willingly make love to me at least once a day. Then I'll let you keep her, for now." He's looking at me in anticipation.

I swallow hard to hold back the bile in my throat. I want to scream at him to let us go and that if he ever lays his body on me, I'll kill him. But, I have to be smart about this if there is to be any chance for Anita and me to get out of here alive.

"I'm not ready yet. If you love me, really love me, you will wait until I am." Maybe that will hold him off until I can figure a way out of this mess.

"No, I don't think so. We've been waiting long enough, don't you think? It's either going to be you or her. You choose."

His face lights up with a manic smile. He turns and picks up the bag that he carried in with him. "I brought you some clothes. It gets cold down here at night. I brought a few extra blankets, as well. I hope you don't mind that I used your fireplace to burn all of your mother's research. Sorry, I know how important her writings were to you, but I couldn't risk anyone finding them and putting two and two together, like you did. I do have to ask if you led anyone to believe that a serial killer is living in our town or that you were thinking it could be me or my father. Let's say, Deputy Walters, for instance. What did you tell him? I watched you and him getting pretty chummy."

I think about how River sat at the table with me while we ate spaghetti and then went over the file. Was Billy watching us from outside? That's why my breath seemed to linger so long on the glass; he breathed on it from the outside. "No, nobody knows anything. How could I tell anyone about you when I didn't even know? Your secret is safe."

I hope that River realizes that I've disappeared and gathers everyone to look for me. I missed my shift at the diner so he must know that something's wrong. I have to hold out hope that someone will find us before Billy kills us. This place must be hidden well away from prying eyes because he's brought other girls here and nobody found them. So how can I really believe that anyone is going to find us? Despair is all I can feel.

"So what do you think, Katie? Will you make love with me? It will strengthen our bond. We will become one, finally. You can't deny that it is our destiny." He asks so sweetly, as if I would even consider his forcing me to have sex with him to be real love.

I look over at Anita and she's staring at me with terror in her eyes. She knows that if I say no, he'll take her. I pace back and forth along the bars trying to use up more time. I figure that the longer I take to respond, the more time it will allow someone to realize what's happened and find us.

His patience wears thin. He persists, "Katie, I'm waiting. I don't want to hurt you. Give yourself to me and promise to be mine forever. If you do, I will be very fair with you. I will never make love to another woman again. But this means that you will stand by my side for all of eternity as my loving partner. I will in turn promise to hold back my urges. I love you dearly, Katie. Tell me that you will consider my offer. Be mine, Love."

What do I do? If I fight him on this, he will either take me anyway or rape Anita, possibly killing her when he's finished. I can't be responsible for her death. Please, please let someone save us before he hurts me.

He yells loudly, echoing my name through the tunnels. "Katie!"

I jerk back from the bars. Angry tears run down my cheeks. Every hair on my body is standing on end. "Yes, fine. Just promise me one thing... that you will never make love to Anita and that you won't kill us. If you agree, I'll do whatever you want." I'm shaking so much that my knees might give out.

CHAPTER 24

My shred of hope that we'll be rescued in time is fading. This is really going to happen. I always thought that my first time would be a wonderful, magical experience with the man I loved, perhaps on my wedding night.

I think being heroic is supposed to make you feel good but all I feel is terrified. I may have saved Anita but at what cost? I've never had sex and now I'm expected to pretend that this is something that I want to do.

"Wonderful! I promise I'll please you." He tosses handcuffs to Anita and orders her to cuff herself to the bars. He hands me a pair and tells me to take off my clothes, lie down then secure my hands to the cot. When I hesitate, he orders me to do it. I jump and drop the handcuffs. "Stop wasting time, Katie."

I slowly pick them up and then remove my shirt and jeans, leaving on my bra, panties and socks. He gestures for me to remove everything. He's watching me with lust in his eyes. My exposed skin instantly chills in the cool air making me shake harder. I feel so forlorn. I take off my clothes but leave on my socks.

I stand before him with my arms crossed over my private areas, trembling. He removes his jacket and shirt without shifting his eyes from my body.

Billy steps closer to the bars. "Now lie down. Be a doll and fasten the handcuffs around the bedpost and your wrists." I tighten it around my one wrist but only pretend to secure it to my other. Hopefully, he doesn't check the cuffs.

He unlocks the door and swings it open. He stands there for a moment looking at my naked body and chewing on his bottom lip. He secures the door then puts the key into his pocket, locking us in together.

Seductively he whispers, "I've been waiting for this for a very long time. I'm so happy that you're here."

He walks over to Anita as he's undoing his pants. She starts crying and begging. "Open your mouth, bitch. If you bite me, I'll kill you, slowly and painfully."

"No! You promised you wouldn't touch her!" I scream. I have to convince him to leave her alone. "Besides, I don't want to share you. If you want to be with me, then you have to be with just me, not her, never her." I can't stand by idly and let him do that to her.

"So you're jealous? You see, you do love me. You didn't realize it until just now, did you? I knew you would see it too. As you wish, my love... just you and me." Billy undoes his pants but leaves them on. He drags his finger tips from my toes to my chin, not missing any sensitive areas. I close my eyes hoping to escape my body and go to a happier place where I can wait for my moment to fight.

I want to leap off this bed and run for my life but I have to bide my time wisely and choose just the right moment when he is at his weakest. Billy slides himself onto me and opens my legs guiding his hips down onto me.

He glides his hand down my thigh resting it under my buttocks. He grinds his crotch into me while kissing my neck and chest. Tears stream endlessly from my eyes. I feel like I'm stuck in a nightmare that's about to get so much worse. Why can't my mind leave me and take me somewhere else, anywhere else?

I can hear Anita praying in the corner. She's whispering quietly but I can hear her every word as if I'm crouched next to her. I feel like I'm in a tunnel where every sound is clear but distant.

I'm snapped back to reality when a piercing pain in my groin rushes through me forcing my body to stiffen. A scream escapes me. He is inside me, holding perfectly still. I want to vomit. My body is writhing, as it's trying to get out from under him. I want to make it stop but I can't, it's too late and his weight is pinning me to the cot. His breath is heavy on my face as he stares into my eyes. I purposely fight to look away from him but his hand holds my chin in place.

The more he moves his hips, the hotter the fire burns inside me. Dreadful noises escape my lips. His weight forces the air from my lungs with every thrust into me. He buries his face in my neck, kissing and licking.

His words are muffled and laboured. "I love you so much, Katie. You love me too. Tell me you love me. We are one now. It's you and me forever. Can you feel our bond?" I say nothing. He keeps whispering.

"I love you. I love you, Katie. You feel so good. Do I feel good, Katie? Am I pleasing you? Tell me you like it. Tell me how much you love me."

His hand releases my face only to grab my breast and squeeze. I wince as more pain floods through my already burdened body. He slams his hips up and down, impaling my inflamed vagina again and again. I cry out hoping for sympathy but it only seems to entice him.

When I don't tell him what he wants to hear, he stops moving his hips and grabs my chin, clutching it firmly. He turns my face to look up at his eyes. "Open your eyes and look at me. I want to see you looking at me." I refuse to meet his eyes.

He once again starts driving himself into me with such incredible force that my body stiffens. It hurts so much. I have no more will to hold them back. I'm getting dizzy. I blink my eyes to try to focus. I force myself to look at him, hoping it will slow down this excruciating attack.

He holds perfectly still. "Tell me you like it. Come on Katie. Tell me how much you love me." He waits for me to speak. I don't think I could even if I had any desire to. I squeeze my eyes shut, no longer giving him what he wants. I just wish he would get off of me. "Open your eyes Katie. Look at me. Look at me or I'll go visit Anita. I'm sure she'll look at me. You know you don't want to share me. Now tell me you love me."

"Okay! I... love... you." I manage to say.

I open my eyes and glare into his, wishing I could set him on fire with my thoughts. Rage is building deep within me. I will not succumb to self-pity. I can't, Anita needs me to be strong. I won't give in to him!

He buries his face in my neck again, kissing and licking me. His hips begin grinding into me once again. Painful heat flares inside me hotter with every thrust. If I don't do something soon, I'm going to pass out. I clutch the handcuff tightly in my hand and swing with all my might, aiming for the top of his head. With a loud thud I hit my mark.

He jerks upward with an expression of disbelief. There's a darkness in his face that I've never seen before. I'm instantly terrified. What have I done?

Having nothing to lose, I swing again, hitting him in the jaw. His left hand covers my face, completely covering my nose and mouth, pushing my head down into the mattress. My nose hurts and I can't breathe. His other hand grabs my left wrist. I have to keep swinging. If I don't, he'll kill me right now.

I remember how my father used to punch my mother in the jaw, rendering her unconscious almost every time. I aim for that spot on Billy's face, again and again. I swing as hard as I can. I don't stop until his eyes flutter, then close.

His full weight crushes down on me, pressing me firmly into the cot. His hand falls from my face. I gasp in a full breath of air letting it escape me with a wail of sheer panic. My mind is rushing. What if I can't get out from under him before he wakes up? He will surely kill me.

Anita is screaming in the corner, "Get up, Katie. Hurry! Help me, Katie. Help me."

I squirm to get out from under his unconscious body. I push his weighty frame with all my might. A panicked rush of adrenaline gives me strength that I've never had. I pull out from under his dead weight, ending up on the floor with my leg still pinned under him. I yank hard to free my remaining limb from its clutch and crawl on my hands and knees trying to get as far away from him as I can. He's going to wake up, I know he is.

I stare at him, astonished that he isn't coming to as I pull my pants on and grab my shirt. Tears stream down my face, dripping from my chin. I reach for Anita and realize that she can't run because she's still cuffed to the bars.

She's pulling at her cuffs, desperate to be free of her shackles but they won't budge. Her eyes are filled with panic. "Katie, help me! Don't leave me here, please!"

I have to find the key. I gasp for breath as I force my legs to walk over to Billy's unconscious body. I dig through his pockets never letting my eyes look away from his face in case I see him twitch. I quickly find the key to the handcuffs then free Anita from her restraints then remove mine.

She thinks to grab a blanket as we run from our prison and down the long dim tunnel. We don't know where we are but we run toward the light. For all we know, we could be running deeper into the tunnel, trapping ourselves. Lucky for us, our instincts were right.

CHAPTER 25

We reach the opening and rush out. It is nearing dusk outside and yet the brightness still stings our eyes, disorienting us. We stagger around, trying to decide which way to run.

We have to put as much distance between us and him as we can, as fast as possible, because we are not going to get very far after the sun goes down.

We don't even know where we are. Which way do we go? What if we run in the wrong direction and are farther lost in the wilderness? Or worse yet, run in a circle, bringing us right back to Billy's dungeon of torture?

Anita pulls on my arm waking me from my rapid-fire thoughts, forcing my legs to move. So we run, not to anywhere in particular, just away from here... away from certain death. I can't help but keep glancing behind us because all I can imagine is Billy right on my heels, grasping at me, with blood and rage all over his face.

The branches clutch at our bare arms and cold faces while we fight our way through the brush. It's so dense at times that we can hardly walk. The dried up weeds and fallen leaves hide the sharp sticks and rocks that pierce our feet, stabbing at our soles. Sock give little protection against the elements. My feet throb with each step. We are starting to leave a blood trail in the shape of footprints behind us. At least with the sun going down and the chill worsening, our feet should numb soon, easing our pain.

It's cold, like the inside of my refrigerator. The temperature is dropping by the minute as the sun falls behind the mountain. In the darkness, we can no longer even see our breaths. The moon is hidden behind deep grey clouds. Even though it isn't blowing, the air nips at our skin.

Anita stops and leans against a huge tree trunk, exhausted. Through panting and tears, she whimpers, "I have to stop. Please. I'm so cold. My feet hurt so much. We can't even see where we're going anymore. If we keep this up, we'll walk off the edge of a cliff or into the den of a wild animal."

"You're right. We need to hunker down somewhere." My teeth are chattering, making it hard to talk. "I'm just thinking that if we do stop, we might freeze to death. I don't know how cold it's going to get." The bitter air bites at my skin.

"I don't care anymore. I'm so tired and so cold. We can keep each other warm with our body heat." Anita is shaking violently to the point that her teeth click together while she talks.

I slide down the tree beside her and wrap the blanket around us both. We feel around to find broken branches and piles of leaves to cover us, not only to keep us warm but to hide the brightness of our white blanket from Billy's sight, just in case he's out searching for us.

If he's conscious, I'm pretty sure he's planning on hunting us down in the morning, if not tonight. I know he's a good hunter because that's what he and his father do to bond; they hunt with bow and arrow. At least, that's what he told me, but I can't be certain of anything about Billy anymore. Maybe hunting animals suppressed his inner demons, restraining him enough so he had no need to hurt people. For all I know, they could have been hunting humans.

Anita and I hold each other, and use our body heat to stay alive. We shiver and shake beneath the blanket and the leaves. We talk about how hungry we are and how much we'd pay for a glass of water and a hot bath. The night is spent sleeping in shifts, listening for wild animals, or worse: Billy.

Every tree looks takes the shape of a human in the darkness. I sit here, for the most part, alone; Anita sleeps beside me. The bushes move in the wind and my mind momentarily panics thinking the worst; a bear, wolf or Billy. I'm sure Anita sees the same nightmarish visions while I take my turn to sleep.

I wake with Anita shaking me. "Katie, we need to start moving. The sun is rising and he's going to be out looking for us soon."

The sun isn't over the mountain yet and we can barely see but she's right, we have to start walking. Billy is probably already tracking us like a hunter would track a deer.

We stagger to our scabbed feet, groaning and wincing in pain. We try to stretch our cramped, stiff muscles. Our bodies have already begun to shiver. Our breath is thick in the air. It's so very cold. I tell Anita to wrap herself in the blanket and we'll switch in a little while.

I just want to lie back down under that blanket until someone comes to find us. But we don't know who that would be. We don't know where we are or if anyone is even looking for us. And, who's to say they'd even be searching in this area?

"We have to get to higher ground. If we can see the mountain ridges, we might be able to get an idea of where we are." I whisper to Anita.

She points in the direction that looks like our best option. We slowly begin to make our way through more brush and over the fallen, half rotted trees. The slope of the mountain is slick with mud in some areas and hard rock covered with slippery moss on others.

Our bodies are resentful of every movement. Despite being cold, I can still feel the rawness of my feet. My bruised vagina hurts with every step, reminding me of the brutal beating it endured. I have cramping inside me that feels like I'm going to start my period even though that's not due for another week. I have to not think about what he did to me. There's no time for self-pity right now. I have to keep moving.

At the peak of the ridge, I see another hilltop that I recognize. It's a mirror image, the back view, but it's the familiar crest that I can see from my backyard. Relief overcomes me and my legs crumple. At least I know where we are but I also know that we have several hours of walking ahead of us. I pray that we will never have to overcome anything more difficult than this.

"We have to go this way." I point toward my house. "I live just on the other side of that summit. From here, it's the shortest distance to any help. There's nothing closer in any direction. We can get there around noon if we really push it. Do you think you can manage?"

Anita stares off in the direction we need to go. Tears run silently down her cheeks as though she has abandoned all hope. Very sadly, she says, "I don't know. I'm tired and cold... so, so cold. But I'll try. I suppose there's no other option. My stomach won't stop growling. I really wish I would have eaten that sandwich now." She sighs.

"Me too." I wrap my arms around her. "Okay, let's go. We can do this." I say as I take her hand in mine and gently pull her along.

We start down the other side of the ridge, tripping and sliding the whole way. At the bottom, a stream quickly flows. We both run to it, dropping to our knees, cupping the near freezing water with our hands and gulping it down. It's extremely frigid. I'm sure the only reason it hasn't solidified into ice is because it's moving so rapidly. My throat aches as I swallow, trying desperately to quench my thirst. I drink until the pain in my hands won't let me cup them any longer to hold more water.

"We have to move. If we stay still, we freeze." My vocal cords are so chilled that I can only whisper with barely a sound. We are both shivering violently now. Maybe the cold water wasn't such a great idea but we were so thirsty.

We run, walk, and crawl. We even wade through thigh deep, bitterly cold water until we reach my house.

We hide in the trees, looking and listening for Billy. We are nearly hypothermic so we don't pause nearly long enough to be sure that nobody is watching.

I grab Anita's hand and we stagger to the house. I pull on the sliding glass door and I'm surprised to find it unlocked. We enter cautiously, keeping our senses sharp. Anita grabs the blanket from the sofa and wraps herself. I grab one from the closet and fight to unfold it with shaking, numb hands. I drop it several times, unable to hang on to it. I run the warm water in the kitchen and put my hands under it. Anita follows my lead.

We cry out in pain as the water warms our digits, bringing them back to life. When I have feeling again, I search for the phone but it's not in its cradle. I look around only to find Jack, lying perfectly still in his bed.

How could I have forgotten about Jack? "Jack... Jack!" He doesn't move a muscle. The phone is lying beside him on his bed next to the couch. I get down on my knees and crawl over to him, hoping and praying that he's just in a deep sleep and didn't hear me come in. I touch his foot but he doesn't move.

With trembling hands, I reach for his chest and hold my hand on his ribs. They don't move either. There is no breath in his body. Jack is dead. My hand is covered in cold, viscid blood. That's why Anita saw blood on Billy and me when he first brought me into the cave. Jack must have fought

Billy just like he did when Billy killed my mother. He lost the battle again, only this time, he gave his life.

I pick up the phone and press 911. When I put it to my ear I hear nothing. The phone is dead. It isn't only the silence from the receiver that alerts me; the death-like stillness in the air makes the hair on the back of my neck stand at attention. Before I even look, I know that something is dreadfully wrong.

CHAPTER 26

I turn to see Billy. He has a white bandage with blood seeping through it on the left side of his head. He has bruises and cuts on his face from where I hit him with the steel handcuff. I gasp; he is not alone.

He stands with a knife against Anita's throat. I'm fixed in my spot terrified that if I move, he'll slit her neck. There's no need for Anita's voice to cry out for help: her eyes are screaming at me loud and clear.

"Please, don't hurt her. If you ever truly loved me, you won't hurt her. You promised me." I beg him.

Everything inside me tells me to charge him but I know that I'll never make it in time to stop him from using that knife to end her life. Her death will be my doing.

"Yeah, see that's where we have a bit of a problem. You promised that you would make love to me every day but then you

316

assaulted me and ran away. So, our deal is off. I've always loved you but you constantly disregarded me as a possible love interest. I told your mom that I was going to marry you one day. She just laughed. I suppose she thought I was joking. I wanted to slap her down then and there but I restrained myself."

"Is that why you killed her?" I ask.

He chuckles, "No. It was months ago that I told her I'd marry you. I already told you that I killed her because she got too close to the truth. She called me on the phone that night and started to explain what she'd discovered. I went over to your house so that we could discuss it further. When I got here, she said that you were already asleep with one of your migraines. She mentioned that you had taken a pill and that we could talk freely because you were out cold and wouldn't hear anything. I know how those pills affect you. Nothing short of a tornado would wake you. I've seen you in that state before. I actually thought about making love to you one night when you were unconscious. I knew you'd never know but figured I'd wait, that you would eventually come to your senses and want me as much as I want you. I knew that one day you'd be mine."

"And I am. I am yours. You did make love to me and I... I belong to you now." I try to say the words as though I mean them but I stutter them out despite my efforts. "You can let Anita go and we'll go wherever you want."

He shakes his head. I had not convinced him of my loyalty. "You love me so much that you beat on me then ran away?" His statement is more a question.

"I'm sorry. I just wanted to get Anita to a safe place so that you and I could be together... alone. I was going to go back to you after I knew she was going to be all right." Again I stutter. "I'm jealous. You said it yourself. I don't want to share you with her. If you let her go, we'll be together forever. I already talked to her and told her not to say anything to anyone. Isn't that right Anita?"

Anita's eyes are locked on mine. She nods her head slightly. "Yeah, I won't tell anyone. I just want to go home. She loves you. She told me."

Billy smiles tersely at me. "Katie, I've known you long enough to know when you're telling a fib. Just stop trying to fool me, it won't work."

"I just don't want you to hurt her." I take one step toward them then hold still. "Tell me about my mom again."

Billy motions for me to stay where I am. "Your mom told me all about her research. At first, she didn't accuse anyone. She just described the coincidences in the dates of the murders and my family's moving from one province to another. Unfortunately she figured out that it all fits within the timeframe of the murders. She was a very good investigator. She should have been a cop."

I inch my way closer to him, all the while looking for something I can use as a weapon. This girl is going to die soon if I don't prevent it. He enjoys killing. I know that nothing I can do or say is going to convince him to let her go. Anita stands straight and tall, hands clenched into fists, obviously too terrified to fight her way out of his grasp. It's up to me to save her.

"So you didn't make love to me the night you murdered my mother? Is that because she caught you trying to? Is that what happened?" I know that's not what happened but I'm just trying to keep him talking to give me more time to think of what to do to help Anita.

Billy continues to reason out why he killed my mother. "No, I wasn't going to touch you that night. I told you that I had decided to wait until you came to your senses and realized that we would make a perfect couple. I didn't even come to your room until I had your mother somewhat incapacitated, but not dead." He takes a deep breath and exhales with a heavy sigh. "I didn't want to harm your mother. Please know that. She seemed like a really nice lady. And you did love her very much. I knew it would hurt you if she were dead. But I also thought that you might throw yourself into my loving arms for comfort. I could shut her up and get you all at the same time. Kill two birds with one stone, so they say."

"Did you have sex with my mother?" I refrain from screaming at him. There would not have been any love making, it would have been nothing short of rape, I'm sure of it. My mother would have fought him with every cell in her body.

"I had to. It's a physical thing. Inflicting pain on someone, having that much control over them, is so exciting. You were upstairs, unconscious. I could have taken you at my will and you would have had no memory of it. Do you have any idea how exciting that is? I was hard as a rock from the thought, like I am right now. Anyway, I needed a release. You and her have the same eyes so it was easy to pretend she was you that I was making love to. It's okay though, she was still alive when I made love to her. It's not like I'd fuck a dead body! That's just gross." He shivers as if the thought repulses him.

He really is sick. A normal person can't fathom his reasoning. He's a psychopath for sure. How did I not know this? How did I walk through the last few years of my life that blind?

"Why did you cut off her finger?" I don't know why I ask that question.

Billy sighs, "I didn't mean for that to happen but she wouldn't stop grabbing at the knife. I didn't technically do it; she did it by hanging onto the blade. I told her to let go but she wouldn't. Sorry about that." He shrugs.

I take another step around the table, still searching for a weapon when he shakes the knife my way. "I think you've come close enough. One more step and the beautiful Anita will no longer be with us. You don't want that to happen, do you?"

Anita's eyes flutter. Tears continue to fall down her cheeks. Billy's hand still holds her chin tightly, stretching her neck. The knife returns to its spot on her throat.

I have to get him away from Anita at any cost. "Why don't you let her go so that you and I can sit down and talk this out? You can tell me everything. In time I'm sure that I can forgive you. You're still my best friend and I'm here for you. Perhaps one day I will grow to love you more... if you'll just give me that chance. But, if you kill Anita, I can't see myself ever forgiving you. She didn't do anything to you and she deserves to have a life. Just... sit with me. Please!"

"No, I have a better idea. Why don't you put on some shoes and a sweater and we'll go back to the cave so we can discuss it there. I promise to leave Anita here. Does that sound like a good idea to you?" Billy asks.

He's being deceitful. "Will you leave her here alive or are you going to kill her? You need to be more specific before I agree to anything."

Billy bursts into laughter. "You'd make a great lawyer because you know how to read between the lines. You see, that's another reason why I love you so much. You're very smart. There's no way that Anita is going to make it out of here alive and you know it. The first thing she'll do is tell everyone who I am and what I've done. There'd be a manhunt for us. You must realize that I can't allow that. I mean... to think that they would put you in jail for willingly being with a fugitive... I can't allow that. I can't bear the thought of someone else putting you in a cage where I can't have access to you."

Anita's face pales. The full realization that he is going to kill her has sunk in. She looks straight at me. I can see the change in her eyes the very second her decision to fight is made. She flinches when he moves the knife to wipe the sweat from his forehead.

As if in slow motion, I launch myself over the coffee table toward them, just as Anita swings her arm, sinking her elbow deep into his belly. The hand around her throat grips tighter, lifting her from the ground. His other hand with the knife drops to Anita's side. Billy growls as the butcher knife slides easily into her ribs.

My fist hits Billy square in the face beside his nose. My other hand pushes Anita. Billy's grip is pulled from her throat as she's hurled onto the sofa and Billy and I fall to the ground in a heap.

He grabs my hair in his left fist pulling me up to my feet as he stands. With his right hand he punches me squarely in the face. There's a moment of confusion and blinking white lights. I can't pass out. If I do, he'll kill us both. Or worse, he'll kill Anita and take me with him. We'll never be seen alive again.

Fear rips through me as I fling my arms about, grabbing and hitting. Again, I'm stunned by another painful blow to my face. This time my body goes limp and I fall to the floor, putting my arm through the glass on the coffee table on the way down. I barely feel any pain from the glass as it slices my arm but the punch to my cheek makes my eye feel like it's going to pop out. The pressure is unbelievable.

Through spinning vision, I watch as Billy slowly pulls the knife from Anita's ribs. He lies over her, between her legs and starts grinding his pelvis into hers. He's dry humping her and groaning with great pleasure. I know that while he's in this vulnerable state, I could kill him, if only I could get the room to stop spinning.

He strokes her face gently, lovingly with his hand then drags the sharp edge of the knife from her left eye all the way down to her jaw leaving behind a trail of blood spilling from the newly formed slit. Even though he's cutting into her face, she barely flinches. Her eyes stare at him as if begging for mercy or for him to just kill her quickly and end her suffering.

Billy kisses her lips and caresses her bleeding cheek before unhurriedly sliding the knife into her abdomen. She cries out in pain as it glides through her belly. He watches her face with an expression of complete adoration. He's truly enjoying this, lost in his own loathsome world. His breathing is rapid. He's very aroused, very susceptible.

I clutch a chunk of glass in my hand but barely feel it shearing through the skin on my fingers and palm. I pull myself up to my knees and try to stand but the world keeps spinning and won't stop. I crumple to the floor again and again. I manage to crawl over to where I can touch Anita's scraped, wounded feet. I reach up and place my hand on her foot. I hope she feels me here. She's going to die a gruesome death and I can't stop it but maybe I can comfort her even the tiniest bit.

Billy turns his face so he can watch me. His body quivers and jerks. With a heavy sigh, he stops grinding on Anita. His orgasm has weakened him for a moment but he quickly gathers his strength and stands up. The expression he wears is of complete satisfaction, as if he has the world at his feet.

"That was exciting and unexpected! Now what am I going to do with you?" He grabs me by my arms and lifts me up, kissing my lips before throwing me over his shoulder. He carries me out of the house. I try to look at Anita to see if she's alive or dead but she blurs as my world spins out of control.

He carries me outside and down the front steps. I can't see clearly because my eyes can't focus. Hanging upside down isn't making it any easier. My stomach clenches and I dry heave. All I can do is hold on to his belt to give me a little stability and say a prayer for Anita. I beg for her to have the strength to stay alive long enough for someone to help her.

The earth is suddenly coming at me very quickly as my face hits the dirt with a painful thud. I see white stars, then blackness.

CHAPTER 27

Mom and I are sitting at the table eating dinner like we always do. She sips her water then smiles at me. I feel so comfortable, truly peaceful. Everything is incredibly bright and warm. I don't remember how I got here but I never want to leave. I feel whole again.

I doesn't seem like I'm in a dream but this is too perfect for it to be real life. For reasons unclear to me, I know I will have to remember every detail of this moment forever. This whole situation seems odd because I don't remember that my mom is dead.

I glance over at her and notice how perfect her skin looks. It is smooth and flawless. Her hair is longer than usual and more flowing. Each strand captures the sunlight. Her eyes are brighter, bluer, almost twinkling. She appears to glow. I don't understand why.

"Katie, everything is going to be all right. Sometimes you'll be faced with challenges that seem too much to bear but you will overcome those difficult times. Great things are going to come your way." My mom smiles the most angelic smile. A feeling of warmth soothes me.

"Mom, I love you." I don't know why I need to say that to her, I just do. "I miss you too." I feel like I should cry but I can't. Why am I unable to cry?

Her presence makes me feel blissful and relieved. That must be why I can't cry. Everything is perfect right now; better than perfect. At this very moment I can't remember anything that's upsetting or troubling me. The only thing that exists is she and I, right here, eating dinner. This is a moment to treasure.

I reach my hand out toward her on the table and she rests hers upon mine. Her skin is so soft and warm that it emits a sense of comfort up my arm. A smile crossed my face. I'm happier than I've ever been.

"Never miss me. I'm here with you all the time. Just talk... I'll hear you. I have to go now and you have a life to live with many lessons to learn. Try not to repeat the mistakes in your life. You are so much stronger than you give yourself credit for. And, always remember that I love you very much." The dream fades away, leaving darkness and sadness. Dread fills my soul. Now I can cry.

"No! Don't go! Come back, please!" I try to yell but it only comes out as a whisper. I know it's over. The dream has run its course. I can't hold onto it. I may never see my mother again.

That wonderful sense of calm and perfection has left me, leaving pain and panic in its wake. The world spins when I open my eyes. Through blurred vision, I see two people but I can't focus on either to know who they are. My mind is still cloudy, still hoping to return to the serenity of a moment ago.

"Katie, you're safe now. You're in the hospital." It's a man's voice. Deputy River Walters, I think.

A female voice is closer to me. She's leaning directly over me. "Katie, open your eyes." I try to but they're so tired that they close against my will. She repeats, "Open your eyes for me, Katie."

Her fingers lift my right eyelid then the left one. I hear the two people talking but then the world drifts to black again. I dream of silly things jumbled into one confusing dream.

Slowly I open my eyes to a dim room. I feel warm and tingly. I'm familiar with the feeling; I'm medicated for pain. I get this way when I take my pain killers for the migraines.

"Katie, how do you feel? It's me, River. You're going to be okay now. You're safe. He's not going to hurt you anymore." His voice is calm and soothing.

My memories of what's transpired are all crashing back. I remember Billy raping me, stabbing Anita, he killed Jack. It's all so clear now.

"Anita?" That's all I can get out between gasping breaths. My throat is so dry. I need a drink. "Water..." The word barely makes a sound.

A straw is placed in my mouth and I suck weakly. A few sips are all I can swallow but it feels like I'm drinking a lake's worth. I focus as best I can on River who appears to be weaving around and blurring in weird ways.

"She's alive. She's in surgery right now. The doctors say she has a good chance for a complete recovery. You are going to be just fine. You have a fractured arm, broken nose and a concussion. The nurse gave you a painkiller but it's probably the concussion making you dizzy. It'll go away soon enough. For now, just rest. We can talk in the morning. I'll be right here until you wake up." River touches my hand.

I force my eyes open and blink several times in an attempt make them focus. It's useless. "Billy?" I ask.

Several seconds of silence fill the room before he speaks. His voice is firm and reassuring."He can't hurt you anymore. Don't worry about him right now. I want you to rest. We can talk about everything when you wake up. Now sleep."

River's warm hand touches my face. My eyes slowly close and I drift into another bizarre dream that involves a big floppy hat, a telephone and me running a marathon while trying to avoid stepping on any one of the millions of thumbtacks that have been spread out on the road. It's just one of those crazy dreams that doesn't mean anything.

CHAPTER 28

It's been a few weeks since River shot and killed Billy before Billy could put me in his car and steal me away forever.

River was just pulling up in his car when he saw Billy carrying me over his shoulder. He said that we both had blood on us and just the way Billy was behaving sent shivers through his body. He could sense something was grievously wrong.

He told me that he had confronted Billy and told him to put me down but Billy kept walking toward his own car. River took out his gun, aimed at Billy and ordered him to stop immediately. He told Billy that he'd shoot him if he kept walking, but Billy wouldn't even acknowledge that River was there.

River said that he is a good shot but was still afraid that he'd shoot me. But, terrified for me, he took aim anyway and shot Billy's leg. That's when he dropped me on my face, breaking my nose.

Billy stood there staring at River for a whole minute as if deciding what to do. Then, he rushed him. River had no choice but to shoot again, this time hitting Billy's left shoulder. River thought it would slow him down but it only seemed to make Billy angrier. He kept charging River, who had no choice but to kill Billy. He shot him once in the heart, instantly ending his life.

River then went on to reveal his undercover assignment. I finally grew wise to the reason nobody knew anything about River Walters' past. Apparently, he's a member of the Royal Canadian Mounted Police's special investigative unit.

He had been investigating Billy's family for some time. It couldn't be prove that Billy or his father killed those girls. Law enforcement needed someone to become a major part of the community but not to stand out and River was the perfect person for the job. He is young and unintimidating, quiet and reserved.

They did have some evidence that either Billy or his father had a part in the girls' deaths but needed more proof before they could make an arrest and get a solid conviction. River was the perfect fit for a small town such as ours since he was raised in one and had a firm grasp on how people in smaller communities behave. Basically, he knew how to blend in.

River had been keeping a close watch on me because I was friends with Billy. Over time, he worried that I'd find out my best friend's family secret, thus at risk of being hurt.

He didn't know that my mother was investigating the killings until after her murder. He said that had he known, he would have told her the truth about his investigation, in hopes that she would stop her own private research. But, knowing how persistent my mom was, she wouldn't have stopped. She would have sent me away and kept digging into the case to find the evidence needed to put the killer away.

When she was murdered, River knew it was only a matter of time before the truth about his undercover position and his investigation into Billy's family would come to light. He needed to find proof quickly before Billy's family became nervous and fled once again.

River also knew that if Billy and his family left this town he could not follow because that would give away his cover. They would surely know that they were being investigated and would disappear during the night. River would have had to hand the case over to someone else so they could slip into an undercover position that would be involved in the lives of the Staple family.

He couldn't find any definitive proof that Billy's family had anything to do with my mom's murder. The last thing he wanted to do was bring Billy or his father in for questioning and be forced to let them go since they would surely get scared and run. He knew that the investigators might never be able to find them again. They had a way of disappearing.

He wanted to tell me everything while we were sitting at my kitchen table that day when we were reviewing the evidence but he knew I would confront Billy thus putting myself in harm's way. He knew Billy would kill me.

Billy's parents are now in jail awaiting trial, owing to their knowledge of Billy's murderous behaviour. The courts are pushing for maximum punishments for both of them because they didn't come forward. They didn't actually hurt the girls but they didn't stop their son either. They knew that he had everything to do with these crimes and did nothing but aid him in covering it up and running when things became too heated.

Billy's parents believed that his dad could find the right medication to suppress their son's vicious, murderous side. They hoped that he could one day live a normal life. They prayed for it every night.

When Billy was angry or felt that his life was out of his control, kidnapping a girl and holding her hostage to do with as he desired, made him feel in control and powerful. This double life allowed him to appear as a regular teenager to everyone around him.

Billy's parents said it was their burden to carry the knowledge that their son was psychotic because it was their job to protect him at all costs. They honestly believed that they would find a cure for him one day and the killings would stop. I suppose they thought that one murdered girl every so many months was the price to pay to keep their son content.

So many lives would have been saved if his parents could have just admitted that something was dreadfully wrong inside their son's brain and that no amount of medication could set him straight. Personally, I hope they rot in prison. They deserve nothing less for enabling their homicidal son.

As for me, I'm healed physically and stay in touch with Anita as often as I can. My life is different now. I'm so much stronger than I was before. I am a writer now, like my mom was. I wrote my story about Billy. Someone had to tell the world about his victims so that they didn't die in vain. Maybe one day it will help a family with a child suffering from an antisocial personality disorder make the right decision to put their child in a facility that will keep him - or her - from harming anyone.

I no longer question the bad things that happen in my life because I believe there is always a reason for everything. If what I lived through hadn't happened, I would never have become who I am today. I am stronger than I ever thought I could be. I am a bestselling author. Had this not happened to me, I would have never known that I had it in me.

I am now twenty-seven years old. I am married to an amazing man whom I would never have considered, had we not been thrown together. River and I now have two children. My life is exactly how it's supposed to be. I am truly happy, despite the rocky start. If I had to thank Billy for anything, it would be for bringing River into my life.

I dream of my mother from time to time. She always appears so happy that she gives me peace of mind. I wish I could see her in my waking hours but I know that it's just like she said; she's always with me. I close my eyes and think of her when things are too difficult. I can almost feel her arms around me helping me through those times.

One day, when it's my time to die, I will be with her again. Until then, I will be happy, no matter what, because that's what she would want for me.

www.ingramcontent.com/pod-product-compliance
Lightning Source LLC
Chambersburg PA
CBHW061322170626
46817CB00001B/269